**WORLD
MYSTERY ACADEMY**

PURSUIT IN PARIS

BY C.S. DOEMNER

For information address Sterling Wade Publishing, 3827 S Carson St Ste 505-25 PMB 2059 Carson City, NV 89701 U.S.A.

ISBN: 979-8-9851831-0-8

In the World Mystery Academy novels, the author desires to introduce her readers to real places (like Paris) and share real facts about things like historical events and foreign languages. The Doemner Family characters are based on the author's own family, but all the other characters and the plot in the story are completely fictional; any resemblance to actual persons, living or dead, or actual events is purely coincidental.

The author also wishes to tackle challenging issues that real people face, like racism. However, this is a work of fiction, written from the author's own limited perspective and may not match the readers' own experiences.

We hope that this book inspires conversations about culture and values from a place of curiosity and compassion. To support the dialogue and discover more educational resources, please visit www.WorldMysteryAcademy.com.

To the real Cora, Jackson and Bradley,
who make every day an adventure.

And to my fabulous readers — we invite you to join our
adventures by following our family as we travel the world at
www.AllOverTheMap.Family.

You can also become one of our Pen Pals at
www.WorldMysteryAcademy.com.

CONTENTS

SECRETS, STONES, SNAILS AND SIRENS

Cora had always dreamed of visiting Paris, but never imagined she would end up eating snails, exploring underground crypts filled with ancient bones, and risking her life to uncover a dangerous mystery while in the romantic City of Lights.

The adventure, like everything else in her life, started with art. Her mother, Mrs. Doemner, was an art historian. A Parisian museum hired her mom to authenticate a new painting before they purchased it, so the museum didn't accidentally buy a fake.

Mr. and Mrs. Doemner decided that they would make the trip to

Paris a long-anticipated family vacation. Today, the third day since the family's arrival, Mrs. Doemner had taken a day off to drag her three children — Cora, Jackson, and Bradley — to visit the Louvre, the world's largest art museum.

Standing outside the huge glass pyramid surrounded by the magnificent golden palace, Cora pulled out her sketchbook, tucked her blond hair behind her ears, and pushed up the turquoise glasses on her nose. She quickly sketched the dramatic grid of glass and metal until her mother hooked her elbow and pulled her through the entrance of the pyramid marked "Entrée du Personnel" and down the escalator.

"C'mon, Cora! Let's go see *her*," Mrs. Doemner squealed, her long brown curls bouncing down her back as they ran through the back corridor, reserved for the museum personnel.

Mr. Doemner and the boys followed their lead, as Mrs. Doemner used her access badge to bring them into the halls of the Louvre, while the rest of the public waited outside in the line.

By *her*, Mrs. Doemner meant the painting of the *Mona Lisa* by Leonardo DaVinci. Cora had seen images of this painting her whole life. Even her brother Bradley, only six years old, knew it thanks to the movie *Mr. Peabody & Sherman*. Now, they were going to see it in person.

As they snaked their way through the grand hallways of the museum adorned with ancient art, Cora shoved the sketchpad into her backpack, and looked around at what had originally been a palace. She imagined herself as a Queen wandering the long marbled corridors, surveying her royal collection of art. When Bradley got too close to a statue of a young boy with a goat, she declared, "OFF WITH HIS HEAD!" in the most majestic voice she could muster. Bradley stuck his tongue out at her, not at all intimidated by his big sister's antics.

After waiting in a long line, the family finally entered the room and stood in front of the Mona Lisa. Cora's jaw dropped — the most famous woman in the world was only two and a half feet tall!

Jackson pushed his wooly blonde hair out of his eyes and wondered aloud if the paints used were oil- or egg-based. A nearby art student overheard his question; her eyes lit up as the two of them got into a discussion about tempera.

Cora kept walking, shaking her head; her brother was the nerdiest ten-year-old she'd ever met.

An hour later, Bradley started complaining about his aching feet, but Cora found herself mesmerized by the colorful beauty of Delacroix's *Liberty Leading the People* (despite Jackson arguing that a topless woman was probably not the best general to lead a revolution).

"Mom, why don't the statues have arms?" Bradley asked as they passed a white marble statue with a womanly torso and wings, but no head or arms.

Mrs. Doemner explained that appendages (like arms or noses) stuck out and were, therefore, prone to being bumped in transit.

"Sometimes, when we move the art, things fall off," she explained.

Cora secretly suspected that tourists, tired after walking over two miles through the Louvre, had taken the arms off of the *Venus de Milo* and the *Winged Victory* in protest. She giggled as she imagined the guards shouting "Hands Up!" and the vandals raising four marble limbs.

Cora came across a quiet wing where the walls and ceilings were gilded with real gold and the glass cases were filled with jewels. It reminded Cora of Ali Baba's Cave of Wonders. She convinced her parents to let her stop in that wing and sketch while they took a guided "Art of the Revolution" tour. She studied the crowns, scepters, earrings, and broaches featuring diamonds, rubies, sapphires, emeralds — an entire rainbow! She selected a bench across from a display with a heavy crown, encrusted with every possible color of gem, set in gold. She opened her sketchbook and began scribbling.

Cora did not bother drawing the actual jewelry. She focused on the stones inside of the crown, each one carefully faceted with perfect planes. Cora shook her head when she imagined these stones buried deep in the earth. Her dad was an archeologist and geologist who looked like a mountain man, with a full beard and shoulder-length brown hair. She had seen these stones when they first came out of the earth, dirty and rough, no more attractive than any other rock. But, an expert's eye could see the value within, and through careful cuts and lots of polishing, each gem became its own intricate work of art.

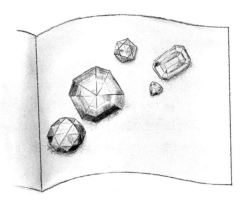

She pulled out her pencils and began filling her page with colorful gems, lost in her own world, until a man's voice startled her from her reverie.

"What a beautiful stone you have there," the deep voice rumbled above her. Cora's head whipped up to see a very tall old man with white hair and round glasses staring down at her. She met his gaze and saw that he wasn't looking at her sketchpad; he was staring at her ring.

Her "mood ring" as she called it, glowed a cheerful shade of green this afternoon. Her father had found the jewel on one of his digs and her mother designed the silver setting; they had gifted it to her on her eleventh birthday. Cora loved it because it shifted colors like a kaleidoscope. Unlike traditional mood rings, Cora's ring didn't seem to be affected by heat or cold; it genuinely seemed to reflect her moods, and sometimes, Cora suspected it did much more than that. At school last spring, one of the "cool girls" with fancy clothes had introduced herself and invited Cora over to her house. Cora eagerly accepted the friendship, but two days later, when she discovered the girl had copied her report and cheated off her test, Cora remembered that the ring had shone black on the day they met.

"Uhh... thanks," Cora replied to the old man. She surreptitiously twisted her ring upside down so only the simple silver band showed and focused again on her art.

The man walked past her to sit down at the far end of her bench and began studying the crown in the case before them.

At first, Cora kept drawing, but her pencil stilled as she noticed a heavy silence had descended upon the exhibit. She looked around. All of the other visitors had left. Even the docent who wandered the halls like a doberman with dentures, was missing.

Cora swallowed.

She could see the old man's reflection in the glass case before her and she studied him, pretending to examine the crown. He had white hair that just touched the rims of his round wire spectacles. He wore a white dress shirt without a jacket, dark jeans and brown leather shoes. Cora could see a gold ring with a large ruby on his left hand out of the corner of her eye. When she glanced back at the case, she got the uncanny sense that he was staring back at her, not the crown.

"Do you often study stones?" he asked, breaking the silence. Cora dropped her pencil in surprise and reached down to grab it, flustered.

"Not as much as my dad," she muttered, once her blue pencil had been recovered from under the bench.

"Oh?" he turned away from the case to look at her directly.

"He's a geologist," she replied to his curiosity. "And an archeologist," she added, because she was proud of him.

His eyes grew wide. "How remarkable! I work with many archeologists. What's his name?"

"Michael Doemner," Cora said unthinkingly, looking at her watch. *Should she leave the exhibit and go find her parents?*

The older man squinted off towards the wall, trying to recollect the name. Finally, he shook his head.

"Nope, the name doesn't ring a bell," he paused to pull out a hand-held device and paused with his stylus hovering over the screen. "How do you spell 'Doemner'?"

Cora gulped. Her mother's reminders of "don't talk to strangers" rang in her ears. And definitely, do not give strangers enough information to Google-search your family, she berated herself. She glanced down at her ring. The green now swirled with smoky tendrils.

"Forgive me," he chuckled when he saw her hesitate. "How rude of me to ask your name when you don't know mine." He reached back into his pocket and pulled out a silver case. The case snapped open and the man handed her a thick, cream-colored card with a swirly, red, deer-looking animal leaping over his name: Theodore Archibald Courteney Devré, E.S.Q.

Cora accepted the card, tentatively.

"Esquire," he smiled, and Cora noticed that his eye color matched her ring. They were sharp and bright and Cora suspected they didn't miss much. "But among friends, I prefer Teddy." He held out his hand. "Pleased to meet you, Miss…?"

"Cora," she answered, setting down her pencil, brushing the eraser crumbs off her palm, and shaking his hand.

"I also love stones," he went on, pointing at her drawings. "I collect them." He took the ruby ring off his finger and offered it to Cora.

Cora's curiosity overcame her trepidation and she took the ring. It was heavy. Really heavy. Delicate ivy wound over the solid gold band and wrapped itself around the blood-red stone. Two tiny deer matching his business card danced on either side.

Cora knew enough about jewels to recognize this rock probably cost a fortune.

"I found this particular specimen on a dig in Burma," he went on, as if reading her mind. "The ancients believed that stones were more than pretty minerals; they had mystical properties that could influence the wearer."

Cora instinctively looked at her own ring. She had never told anyone of her suspicions that her own stone held a secret power.

Teddy caught her gaze and asked, "May I…?" pointing at her ring.

Sudden terror gripped Cora's chest. Why was he so fascinated by her ring? *Don't be silly*, she reassured herself. *What's he going to do? Run away with it? We're in the most heavily guarded Art-Prison in the world.*

Cora reluctantly slipped her ring off her finger. It now blazed red, even brighter than Teddy's jewel.

Teddy's eyes widened. "Fascinating," he whispered. Despite her fear of being separated from her treasure, Cora was secretly pleased by his reaction.

Just then, Cora noticed her family returning to the far end of the hall. Her father caught her eye and waved to her to come join them.

"I've gotta go," she said to Teddy, handing him his ring and taking her own back. She quickly slid it back onto her finger, tossed her pencils into her case and threw the case and her sketchpad into her backpack. "Nice to meet you!" she said over her shoulder as she hurried away.

Teddy's eyes never left her hand, but he waited until she turned the corner before he pulled out his phone to make a call.

• • •

That night, the family went to see an old friend of Mrs. Doemner's for dinner. She had met *Monsieur* Auguste Bocuse when she was a young college student studying art in Paris. He had just launched his hole-in-the-wall restaurant next to the tiny apartment where Mrs. Doemner stayed with three other exchange students.

"Apparently his restaurant has improved since I studied here! He was even reviewed in *Cuisine Magazine*! How fun to see my old friend on a magazine stand in the States! He has invited us for dinner, and I am certain it will be a real treat," Mrs. Doemner beamed as they wandered along the River Seine towards her friend's restaurant.

Cora loved hearing the sounds of French words ringing around her. She thought that the hard R's sounded like someone trying to clear their throat. She had taken a year of French in school and listened for any words she could remember from her class: *marché* was market, *pommes* - apples, *oiseaux* - birds.

They crossed the Pont Neuf, and the sun sparkled on the water as the river boats trolled under the bridge.

"Pont Neuf means New Bridge," Jackson explained to Bradley. "But, it's the oldest bridge in Paris." Jackson only enjoyed non-fiction books and seemed to retain every piece of data he read.

They turned a corner into a smaller street, where rows of striped awnings hung overhead. There were round tables covered by red and white checkered tablecloths, with people sitting outdoors, enjoying the evening. Mrs. Doemner glanced at the address on her phone and announced, "This is it! My, oh my, Auguste has certainly moved up in the world!"

The sun began to descend into the river behind them as they passed the outdoor diners and walked in through the wrought-iron doors. Cora's eyes grew round as she took in the red velvet walls and the candle-lit tables. Shiny black-and-white floor tiles reflected the elaborate white chandeliers. An accordion player stood just in front of the large front windows which read "Chez Bocuse" in gold font. His high-pitched rendition of *La Vie En Rose* transported Cora back to the Paris of her dreams.

A waiter, called a *garçon* in French, rushed towards them. He wore black pants and a crisp white button up shirt. He carried a small tray and walked as if he had springs attached to the bottom of his shoes.

"You must be zhe DOME-NER family!" he announced as he approached them with open arms. Cora noticed he worked very hard to pronounce "DOME-ner."

He whisked them off to a table in the center of the dining room, set with a vase of red roses. "This table eez special for you, courtesy of Monsieur Bocuse himself! He has prepared a menu for you, and he hopes that you will find it delicious. He will be out to visit you in person as soon as he can."

Cora felt a bit conspicuous as plates of food poured out of the swinging kitchen doors to arrive at their table as if they were royalty. They started with *escargot* as an *hors-d'oeuvre*. Bradley's nose curled when he saw the snail-shells on the plate.

"They don't taste as horrible as you'd think," Jackson commented as he chewed on the small rubbery brown ball.

Bradley picked up the miniature fork that came with the shells, dug deep into the gastropod, and tugged. The slippery snail shot out of the shell and flew across the dining room, leaving his tiny silver catapult quivering empty in Bradley's hand. His eyes grew very wide, and he slowly lowered his hands under the tablecloth, hoping no one would slip on the small booger-shaped object now lying in the corner.

When dessert arrived — smelly cheese with freshly sliced pears — Mr. Doemner held up his camera to snap a photo: "Say *fromage!*" Just as he snapped the photo, Monsieur Bocuse arrived for a photo-bomb. He leaned in between Mrs. Doemner and Jackson, a huge grin beaming from under his grey mustache.

"Auguste!" Mrs. Doemner squealed, and she jumped out of her seat to greet her now-famous friend. *"Bonjour!"* he cried, kissing Mrs. Doemner on both of her cheeks the way they do in France.

Cora thought his moustache looked a bit like a mouse, wriggling over his lip as he spoke. He then grabbed Mr. Doemner's hand and shook it several times up and down, as if pumping water. He asked them about Mrs. Doemner's work, and the adults started talking about boring art stuff.

The Doemner children were used to tuning out art talk. Bradley lined up the salt and pepper shaker, making shooting sounds as if the condiments were at war. Jackson, eye-level with the large white buttons on the chef's belly, tried to listen, but he kept glancing at his smart watch, wondering how soon he could politely start playing Sudoku.

Cora stared around the restaurant amazed that after years of wishing, she was finally living a *Parisian* life. She continued eavesdropping on conversations at the other tables to see if she could recognize any French words, determined to go back to school looking as sophisticated as these French ladies who sat around her sipping champagne and discussing duck confit.

Bradley, having killed off both the pepper and the salt shaker, smiled at the two elegant, white-haired ladies next to him — who just happened to be enjoying a slice of *gâteau,* the bistro's famous seven-layer chocolate and raspberry cake. He licked his lips, and the women returned his mischievous grin. One of them, with a silver bun at the base of her neck and a wide smile, wiggled her finger towards him, inviting him to their table for a bite. Before his parents could object, Bradley seated himself at their table, an honorary *petit fils.* Chocolate crumbs fell onto his t-shirt to peals of laughter from the women, who kept handing him forkfuls of the stuff.

Cora took a deep breath and leaned back in her chair, allowing the musical sounds and the delicious aromas to waft around her. Her fingers itched for her pencils, but not even she could capture this perfect moment on paper.

Just then, sirens broke through her mood, quiet at first, then louder and louder, until they stopped right in front of the window. Flashing lights lit up the inside of the dining room, causing all of the patrons to swing their faces towards the commotion. A small blue and white car blaring its warning screeched into the driveway on the side of the restaurant, clearly headed to the back of the restaurant. Police! Her stomach clenched. *What was going on?*

Everyone in the restaurant stopped talking and started whispering behind their hands to the others at their tables. No one was eating anymore, not even Bradley, a forkful of forgotten cake hanging from his fingers, his mouth wide open.

Monsieur Bocuse's forehead wrinkled in concern and the grey animal on his top lip quivered. He nervously excused himself - "*Excusez-moi*"- before running back into the kitchen. The swinging doors bounced back behind him.

Cora craned her neck to try to see in the kitchen. The waiter who had welcomed them earlier and served their meal stopped the doors from swinging and stood taller as if to make a speech. He plastered a fake smile on his lips and shouted at the patrons in French. Finally, turning to the Doemners, he added in English: "EETS OKAY! EETS OKAY! Pleeze… feeneesh your mealz! Eet's a-nothing!"

Cora could see the waiter did not believe the words coming out of his own mouth, but she couldn't see into the kitchen, where shouting had begun. Mr. Doemner asked the waiter for the check, and the waiter refused, "NON! Monsieur Bocuse insisted. His gift to you! Pleeze, enjoy your day in Paris!" He pointed to the door, hinting that it was time to go.

"I wonder what happened?" Mr. Doemner said as he placed several paper *euros* on the table as a tip. Shrugging his shoulders, he added, "We probably should get going back to the hotel."

The voices in the back were now shouting. Cora, Jackson, and Bradley looked at each other, eyes wide. They did not get up. The action in the back of the restaurant glued them to their seats.

"I hope everything is alright," said Mrs. Doemner, her voice tinged with worry. Mrs. Doemner had a hard time walking away from situations where someone might need help. She burned with a curiosity that could kill a thousand cats (and enough compassion to bring them all back). Cora felt exactly the same. She squirmed in her seat, wanting to follow the sound of clanging pots and pans from behind the swinging doors.

"You're friends with Monsieur Bocuse, right, Mom? Can't you go back there and talk to him? Maybe he needs our help!" Cora implored.

Mrs. Doemner looked at Mr. Doemner with raised eyebrows, as if to say, "What do you think?" and Mr. Doemner shrugged back

"Why not?" They pushed back from the table, saying, "You guys stay here. We'll be right back."

But, as you might have guessed, Cora, Jackson, and Bradley were not the "sit tight" types. As soon as their parents disappeared through the swinging doors, Cora stood up and said, "Okay, let's go."

Jackson hesitated, weighing the cost of being caught against the satisfaction of learning more. Bradley just stood up, ready to march into the kitchen. Cora grabbed his arm and stopped him, "Bradley, hold on! We can't just go barging in... Jackson, come on. You know you want to go, too. We'll be smart about it and make sure no one sees us."

Jackson relented, and the three linked hands. They tiptoed and stood to the side of the swinging doors. Cora waited until the *garçon* came back out through the doors, trying to manage the customers who were still murmuring in excitement. He didn't notice the three American kids crouched down behind him. Cora caught the door before it closed shut, took a quick peek, and slipped inside with Jackson and Bradley hot on her heels.

The lights, sound, and smells of the kitchen hit Cora like a frying pan to the face. Unlike the golden lighting and subtle smells out front, the kitchen blazed with bright fluorescent bulbs. All the aromas of raw fish, charred steak and dishwashing detergent made her nose crinkle.

Large, steel workbenches filled the middle of the kitchen with silver pots and cast-iron pans hanging from the ceiling. Stoves and ovens lined the left wall. Floor-to-ceiling refrigerators covered the opposite side. At the back of the kitchen, two uniformed police officers were holding the arms of a young woman with a purple scarf tied tightly over her hair and neck, above a rumpled white kitchen uniform. Tears ran down her dark brown face and she kept shaking her head. The kids ducked under one of the workstations and began to inch their way closer.

Next to the girl, a very short man wore a very tall hat held up by dozens of tiny white pleats. He spoke loud and fast in French. He pointed between the girl and a large walk-in refrigerator with wide open doors. Cold air creeped out in wispy tentacles across the red tile floor.

Monsieur Bocuse kept looking back towards the dining room and making shushing noises, waving his hands to try and calm down the irate chef. His face showed panic and shock.

Cora tried to get closer, creeping carefully around stacks of ceramic dishes. Jackson trailed closely behind her, with Bradley following behind his older siblings. Just when Cora thought they would get away with their espionage, Bradley 'Bull-in-a-China-Shop' Doemner put his hand on the edge to steady himself and jostled a mixing bowl. It fell with a loud clang, dropping freshly whipped cream onto Bradley's head on the way down. Everyone in the kitchen turned to see what the source of the noise was, only to see Bradley with whipped cream pouring down his face.

All three kids cringed. So much for Hide-and-Sneak.

CHAPTER DEUX

FUNGI AND A (NOT-SO) FUN GUY

Cora clapped her hand over Bradley's mouth in case he started to cry. Jackson gulped.

The trio crouched under the kitchen counter, hoping that commotion in the back of the kitchen would keep the adults from noticing them.

Two sets of adult legs walked over to their hiding spot. Long, brown curly hair emerged from above the counter, followed by their mom's face, right next to their dad's head. "Umm... Boo?" Mrs. Doemner teased, not quite sure what else to do in the face of her three children who looked like they were in some bizarre wrestling match.

Mr. Doemner, however, did not look pleased. "I told you guys to stay at the table," he frowned. "Come on out, so you don't get Monsieur Bocuse's dishes dirty."

"Too late," Mom muttered, as she hauled a slimy Bradley out from under the counter, slipping a little on the spilled cream on the floor.

"We wanted to see what was going on," Cora explained, adjusting the turquoise glasses on her nose. She hated being treated like a child. Bradley was the child, not her. *Look at him. He ruined everything.*

Bradley, oblivious, licked the cream from on his face, "Guys, this is really good," he said as he licked it from his hands.

Cora stared daggers at him as their mother grabbed a towel from a hook and started wiping him down with it. She grabbed another one, and threw it at Cora saying, "Help me clean this up off of the floor, please."

The four fixed the mess, while the loud argument continued on the other side of the kitchen. Bradley's little mishap didn't even seem to stop it.

"What are they saying, Mom?" Jackson asked, pointing over at the police who were asking the distraught girl lots of questions.

Mrs. Doemner, wiping the last of the cream from Bradley's face, pulled the kids closer and off to the side so they could see without drawing much attention to themselves.

"It seems," she whispered, "that young lady over there may have stolen some truffles."

"Trifles?" Bradley asked, his tongue still licking his lips, seeking any remaining whipped cream.

Mr. Doemner cracked a wry smile, "No, if it were only a trifle, she wouldn't be in so much trouble." Mrs. Doemner shook her head at the bad 'Dad' joke.

"Truffles are a type of mushroom," Mr. Doemner amended.

"That girl is in trouble because she stole *mushrooms*?" Jackson gasped. He hated mushrooms. "Why would anyone steal mushrooms? More to the point: Why would anybody care if someone stole mushrooms?!"

"These are very special — and very expensive — mushrooms. Evidently, a couple of pounds of white truffles have disappeared. They cost the restaurant over 4,000 Euros," Mrs. Doemner translated, still keeping her voice lowered to avoid interfering with the chaos in front of them.

Bradley's eyebrows shot up and his jaw dropped down. "Mushrooms cost four-thousand DOLLARS??" he shouted so loud that Mrs. Doemner winced.

"European countries use the 'Euro' not the dollar, so technically, it would be even more than four-thousand dollars," Mr. Doemner interjected.

"MORE?! But why are they so expensive?" Bradley pressed. He didn't really know how much that was, but he felt confident that he could buy quite a few sets of Legos with that kind of money.

"They are so expensive because these mushrooms can't be farmed. They can only be hunted in the wild under certain trees at certain times of year," Mr. Doemner explained.

Bradley's eyes grew wide as he imagined stalking wild mushrooms through the forest at night. He would definitely need a bow and arrow to be a mushroom hunter.

Cora had been very quiet, watching the girl who now seemed quite desperate. "What's she saying, Mom?"

Mrs. Doemner listened for a moment, then translated: "She says she would never do such a thing to Monsieur Bocuse. He's the only one who gave her a chance." Mom's eyes started to tear up in sympathy.

"Oh, poor thing," she added under her breath.

"What does that mean — only Monsieur Bocuse would give her a chance?" Jackson asked.

Mr. and Mrs. Doemner looked at each other as if to see if the other might know how to explain what was happening to their children. Mrs. Doemner twisted her lips and raised her shoulder in a shrug.

"Well," Mr. Doemner began, "some people are incredibly prejudiced against Muslims. In France, people have even tried to ban the wearing of *hijabs*." He gestured around his head to indicate the girl's headscarf.

"Prejoo-what?"

"Prejudiced," Mrs. Doemner said, tight-lipped. "It's when a person dislikes someone else without even knowing them and thinks they're bad. Usually because they look different or come from somewhere else."

"Well, that stinks," Bradley stated.

"Indeed," Mom agreed. "Evidently no one else would hire her."

Cora couldn't take her eyes off the girl. She tried to put herself into her position.

How would she feel if someone had accused her of stealing? Cora always worried people wouldn't like her, but the idea that people would hate her just because she wore the "wrong" clothes made her stomach flip. The red tiles of the floor seemed to sway, a blood-red ocean threatening to wash the girl away. Cora decided to throw her a life line.

"I don't think she did it," she said out loud.

Her mom and dad looked at her. "Why do you say that, Cora?"

Cora scrunched up her nose, thinking hard. "I don't really know," she finally admitted. Although she couldn't find the words, she felt it in her bones that the girl standing in front of her was innocent.

"How might you explain it if you *did* know?" Mom pressed.

Cora rolled her eyes and found herself twisting the silver ring on her finger. It reflected the red of the tiles.

"I think my ring is telling me that there is something very wrong happening. And it isn't her fault."

Mr. Doemner's lips curled as if holding in a smile watching his daughter consult jewelry for an answer, but Mrs. Doemner took Cora's ring seriously.

She nodded. "And what else did you notice?"

Cora breathed out a sigh. Sometimes it was just so hard to explain things to adults. How could she help them see things her way?

She looked back at the girl. "Well, when Jackson and Bradley try to hide the fact that they steal candy, they get quiet and stare at their toes. She's crying, so I'd say she's sad, but she's looking the chef and the police in the eye and talking openly when they ask her questions."

The family turned to watch the girl with an intensity that matched Cora's.

"Sure enough," Mr. Doemner said, after a while. "Cora's right. She seems surprised and upset, but doesn't look like she's hiding anything."

Mr. and Mrs. Doemner moved a little closer to the group, shepherding the kids behind them, but Cora's blue eyes and Jackson's brown peeked around their waists, while two hazel eyes peered out from in between Dad's legs.

The scene had reached a fever-pitch, with the small chef red in the face from shouting accusations at the girl, now on her knees, clasping her hands together and begging Monsieur Bocuse for mercy.

Monsieur Bocuse sighed and held up his hands in exasperation, shaking his head. The police stepped forward, slapping handcuffs onto the girl's wrists, and dragging her to her feet. The girl's face

had an expression of pain mixed with fear. Cora thought her heart
might explode.

"Stop!" Bradley shouted, clawing his way between his dad's legs.
He ran to the girl and threw up his arms as if protecting her from
the police. He barely reached her waist, and his tiny frame looked
even smaller in front of the grown bodies in front of him. The girl
looked down at him through tears, her eyes surprised.

"You can't take her away! She didn't do it!"

Everyone halted, staring down in shock at the little blond boy in
a bright red Hawaiian shirt who had just cannonballed into their
midst, shouting at them in English.

Mr. and Mrs. Doemner blushed and apologized to Monsieur
Bocuse as they came forward to grab Bradley.

"*Je suis désolée, c'est ma faute,*" Mrs. Doemner choked out to
Monsieur Bocuse.

Mr. Doemner, who didn't speak French, explained, "I'm sorry
to intrude, Auguste, we came to offer assistance. We didn't intend
to intervene."

They took Bradley's hand and started to lead him back into the dining room, but Cora stopped them. If Bradley could be that brave, so could she. She would not leave this girl alone at the mercy of the men surrounding her.

"We can't let them take her," she declared. "I told you, she's innocent!"

"Oh, sweetie, we have no way to prove that," Mrs. Doemner answered, clearly torn between a desire to get involved and the instinct to avoid further embarrassment by escaping back into the dining room.

"Mom, please…" Cora stammered.

"The Chef de Cuisine seems quite certain she was the culprit," Mr. Doemner pointed out, although he looked like he doubted his own words.

"But we can't let them put her in jail for *mushrooms*!" Cora countered. "That's not fair!"

"I don't think they're taking her to jail," Mrs. Doemner speculated, looking back at the girl. "Would they?" She turned to Mr. Doemner for confirmation, hoping he would know.

He shrugged. "I don't know how the French justice system works. Maybe she just has to pay a fine?"

Jackson, who evaluated the situation as only Jackson could, interjected, "Well, if it's just a matter of money, can't we help her? Can't we just pay for the mushrooms, or something?"

Mr. and Mrs. Doemner looked like he had thrown a bucket of ice water in their faces. "Uh…" Mr. Doemner hesitated.

"My love, that's a lot of money to pay for non-existent fungi," Mrs. Doemner apologized. "We don't even know her."

Jackson shrugged, but Cora remained undaunted. Despite the fact that two police officers and a small army of kitchen staff members were staring at them, Cora made her case: "No, Mom, I know she's innocent. I can't explain why yet, but maybe, if we had a few days, we could figure out what really happened. Maybe even find the truffles! That would be better for Monsieur Bocuse, wouldn't it? And then she could keep her job."

Mrs. Doemner looked helplessly at Mr. Doemner. He ran his fingers through his chin-length brown hair, looking into the eyes of each of his small offspring and sighed.

Turning to Monsieur Bocuse, he asked: "Monsieur Bocuse, if we offered to cover the cost of the missing truffles, would you feel comfortable dropping the charges against…?" he gestured towards the young lady in handcuffs.

Cora took a deep breath, and the floor stopped swaying. If her dad was on her side, they'd be okay.

The kitchen fell silent. Jackson could tell who spoke English, because they stared at the Doemners with hands covering their mouths. The ones who didn't speak English kept glancing between the Doemners and the people with hands on their mouths, trying to figure out what in the world had just been said.

Monsieur Bocuse's eyes widened. "You would do that? For someone you've never met? *Pourquoi?* Why?"

Mr. Doemner shrugged as if he weren't quite sure why he was doing it either. He looked back at the kids and said, "I guess I want to teach my kids that people are more important than money." Mrs. Doemner's eyes welled up again as she drew Cora close in a side embrace.

The small chef in the tall hat seemed offended by the suggestion.

"Zhou cannot come in here and zink to buy off French justice with your dirty American dollars! For this…" he spat out a word in French that Cora didn't understand, while pointing at the girl in the *hijab*. His thin black moustache quivered under his big red nose, and his double-breasted chef's coat strained at the buttons covering his large belly. Although he was in charge of the kitchen, he didn't have a speck of food anywhere on him, and he carried a thin boning knife in his left hand.

Mrs. Doemner blushed as red as the beets on the cutting board behind her, and Mr. Doemner looked about ready to challenge the diminutive man to a duel.

"What did he say?" Cora asked them, quietly.

"He just called her a very bad name," Mrs. Doemner said, shaking with anger.

Mr. Doemner started walking towards the chef, but Monsieur Bocuse intervened. "*Non*, Pierre… my American friends are right. If they are willing to pay for the truffles, then there is no crime, merely a purchase."

He turned and explained the situation to the police, who didn't seem to speak English. They asked a few questions, then bewildered, unlocked the girl's handcuffs.

The girl stared at the Doemner family in disbelief and gratitude.

Pierre, the Chef de Cuisine, also glared at them, grinding his teeth, chewing on words he wished to utter and turning at last to yell at his kitchen staff: "*Allons-y!*" he shouted (*"Let's go!"*). He shooed them back to their work stations with a long string of barked commands in French, occasionally waving the knife around like an ominous exclamation point.

3

CHAPTER TROIS

SAVING JOAN OF ARC

Mr. Doemner followed Monsieur Bocuse to his office to buy the most expensive piece of nothing in history. The rest of the Doemner family moved towards the back door of the kitchen to get out of the way of the bustling staff.

Cora watched as a tall blond cook with blue eyes came up to the girl to make sure she was okay. When the girl nodded, he returned to his station, but Cora caught him glancing back from time to time, just to check on her. He seemed kind and concerned.

The girl walked up to the Doemners, keeping her large dark eyes looking at the ground. "*Merci beaucoup*," she said quietly in French, then repeated a little louder in English: "Thank you very much."

She rubbed her left wrist, as if wiping off the feel of handcuffs. "I don't know what I…" she paused, searching the ceiling tiles for answers. "My family really needs me," she finally finished as tears rolled down her cheeks.

Mrs. Doemner smiled, "*À votre service*. You are most welcome." She reached out her hand. "*Je m'appelle*, Caitlin Doemner."

"I am Jeanne Mokhtari," answered the girl as she shook Mrs. Doemner's hand in return.

Bradley repeated the girl's name with a confused expression: "John? Her name is John?!"

"Her name is spelled 'J-E-A-N-N-E' but she pronounces it 'Jzhon'. Like if you said 'John' while sneezing," Mrs. Doemner explained.

"You speak English?" Jackson asked the girl.

Jeanne smiled shyly and shrugged. "Not very well. I studied it a little in school."

"You speak much better English than I speak French," observed Cora, who thought Jeanne extremely brave. "I'm Cora," she said, sticking out her hand. But before Jeanne could take it, she turned to look at her mom. "What did you say...?"

"When you're introducing yourself, you say '*Je m'appelle*', which means 'I call myself' and then you add your name."

Cora nodded, turning back to Jeanne and stuck out her hand again. "*Zhur muh pell*, Cora," she pronounced with a smile.

Jeanne grinned and shook her hand, "*Je m'appelle*, Jeanne. *Enchantée* - nice to meet you. More than nice. You saved me."

"I saved you," Bradley interjected. "I'm Bradley!" Instead of holding out his hand, he held up his face with duck-lips, waiting to be kissed. Cora rolled her eyes.

Mom laughed out loud. "Oh, Bradley, I don't know if *Mademoiselle* Jeanne…", but stopped when she saw Jeanne bending down to gently touch her right cheek to Bradley's and then switching to touch his left with her left.

Bradley made an elaborate kissing sound both times, which made Jeanne giggle. Her whole face brightened when she smiled.

"Bien sûr! Of course! *Bises* for the hero who ran to my rescue," she said with a grin, her black eyes sparkling.

"And this is Jackson," Mom introduced her middle child by placing her hand on top of his blond curls.

"Are you sure ZHAHN isn't a boy's name?" Jackson asked.

Again, Mom blushed and Cora tried to kick him in the shins, but he moved away. "What?" he demanded.

"That's rude," Mom murmured, but Jeanne interjected, "No, it's fine. I understand that 'Jeanne' sounds almost like 'John'. My mother named me after the French heroine — Jeanne D'Arc."

Cora turned her head to one side. "Wait… Do you mean Joan of Arc?"

"*Oui,*" Jeanne looked at the children and said to Bradley, "That means YES." He repeated the word: "WEE."

"That's so cool." Cora's eyes now glowed with admiration, as if Jeanne really were the famous young girl who had saved the French King (and probably France itself) by leading armies into battle.

"You know our Jeanne?" Jeanne asked, surprised.

"Oh yeah! Mom and I love studying fierce women in history… and she was the fiercest! Did you know she was the general of an army when she was only 17?" Cora replied.

Jeanne smiled again, "I did know that! I'm so glad to find myself among fellow historians!"

"My Dad's a hysterian," Bradley chimed in. Mom snorted in laughter.

"No, Bradley, he's an ar-chae-olo-gist," Jackson corrected, working hard to articulate around his lisp.

While museums hired Mrs. Doemner to verify art pieces, Mr. Doemner examined ancient artifacts, like knives, pottery, even mummies. Bradley loved to tell his school friends that his dad found treasures in mud.

Just then, Mr. Doemner returned, followed by Monsieur Bocuse whose eyebrows were still knitted together. He walked up to the small circle and cleared his throat. "I want to say Thank You, Cait-a-leen, as I have already expressed to Mich'el. I would have offered such a solution myself, but things are... rather hard right now, I'm afraid," he lifted his hands.

Cora crossed her arms over her chest. *What kind of guy threatens to send a girl to jail for mushrooms?* She didn't trust Monsieur Bocuse.

"It is always our pleasure to help our friends," Mrs. Doemner said, reaching out to squeeze his shoulder. Cora gave her a side-eye.

Monsieur Bocuse, not noticing Cora's incredulous look, smiled as tears appeared in his eyes, clearly touched by her gesture. As he looked up, he noticed Jeanne. His eyes widened and he took a step back in shock. "Jeanne, you are still here?" he demanded.

Everyone got quiet. Mrs. Doemner looked at the floor. Mr. Doemner looked at the ceiling. But Cora looked the Frenchman right in the eyes.

"Why wouldn't she be here?" Cora challenged. "Doesn't she work here?"

Monsieur tugged at the collar of his shirt, like it was too tight. "I, uh, well…" He cleared his throat again and his face grew red. "It's just that I don't know if the, uh, staff, would understand if we kept her on," he finished out of breath.

Cora saw the weakness in his face and heard the fear in his voice.

Wow. He is a coward, she thought. She looked at him even harder, hoping to burn a hole in his forehead.

Jackson figured it out first. "You mean you're firing her?"

Monsieur tried to smile, but it looked more like a grimace. "I'm afraid so. *Désolé*, Jeanne," he apologized to the girl whose copper skin looked unnaturally pale.

She swallowed and nodded vaguely. "*Je comprends.*"

Cora's skin felt too tight. *What's happening here? Everyone is just going to go along with this?* "Well, I don't understand!" Cora exclaimed, her face hot.

Mrs. Doemner shushed her, nervously looking back at the dining room.

"She didn't steal your stupid mushrooms!" Cora paused, then looked at Jeanne, looking deep into her eyes: "Did you?"

"*Non!*" Jeanne shook her head vigorously, and pressed her hands up to her face to hide the tears which had begun to fall following the tracks of the ones that had already dried.

"See!" Cora pointed at Jeanne as if the tears proved her case.

Monsieur Bocuse squirmed as if his clothes were very itchy.

"Yes, I also want Miss Mokharti to be innocent," he answered. "But I cannot keep someone who has been accused of stealing. Can you imagine how it would look to my team if we simply... How do you say it in English? Sweep it under the carpet?" Monsieur Bocuse stuttered.

"Rug. Sweep it under the rug." Mrs. Doemner couldn't help correcting him under her breath before turning to Cora. She bent down to look her daughter in the eye. "Sweetie, I know you feel she's innocent, and we always want to think the best of everyone, and thanks to you guys, she's been cleared of charges, but just think how you would feel if you thought Jackson had stolen your purse and we pretended like nothing had ever happened. Even if we replaced the purse, would you feel like that was fair?"

Cora hated it when her mom tried to get her to see both sides of a situation. Cora's mouth scrunched into a tiny scowl. Her sense of injustice felt trapped: it wasn't fair to punish someone for something they didn't do. And she had to admit that she wouldn't feel great if she thought someone got away with doing something wrong. But Jeanne wasn't guilty! Cora simply lacked proof.

Bradley, already attached to Jeanne, impulsively slipped his hand into hers and gave it a squeeze. Jeanne looked down at him with a tear-soaked smile.

Jackson spoke up. "Well... What if we *could* prove she was innocent, Monsieur Bocuse? Could she stay then?"

Hope crested on their faces like a sunrise. Frowns became smiles and eyes grew bright on every face except Monsieur Bocuse's. He reminded Cora of a bunny rabbit startled by a flashlight on a dark night. He blinked. His mouth opened, then closed, like a fish out of water.

Mr. Doemner seemed to comprehend what an uncomfortable position his children had placed their friend into and interceded. "Hey guys, I don't know how that's going to be possible. We're leaving in three days. We were planning on going to Euro-Disney tomorrow…" He trailed off, as if laying a trail of cookies, enticing them away from the situation.

"Yeah! Disneyland!" Bradley took the bait. He let go of Jeanne's hand and shot his pointer-fingers into the air and wiggled his hips in his characteristic Epic-Rock-Dance-of-Glee.

Even Jackson looked willing to give up the chase.

Cora stood her ground. "No," she decided. "This is more important than Disneyland." She looked at Bradley, who found it hard to believe that ANYTHING could be more important than Disneyland. He looked back at Jeanne, and glumly tucked his gun fingers into the holsters of his pockets.

"Monsieur Bocuse," Cora turned to look up at the tall man. "If we can figure out who really stole the truffles before we leave on Friday, will you let Jeanne keep her job?" Her blue eyes burned into his green ones, and he looked away first.

He rubbed his palms against his white pants with black pin-stripes, and finally nodded. "Okay," he sighed. "If you can prove someone else stole the truffles, I would of course, be happy to keep Jeanne on."

Cora grinned, her brothers looking unsure if they should be happy or disappointed.

Bradley broke the silence. "So... no Disneyland??"

4

CHAPTER QUATRE

PIG DETECTIVES, AT YOUR SERVICE

The family wrapped themselves around Jeanne and swept her out of the restaurant towards the Métro, Paris' underground subway system. Cora's mind raced: How could she prove someone else had taken the truffles?

Cora wrote Jeanne's phone number in her sketchbook. She then ripped out the page that had a drawing of a sapphire from the French King's crown and wrote her parents' numbers on it. Jeanne admired the drawing and thanked Cora for giving it to her. The Doemners promised to keep Jeanne informed, and they all said good-bye to each other, not quite sure what to do next. Cora's heart followed Jeanne down the stairs to the subway.

Darkness had fallen and the River Seine looked like a black velvet ribbon studded on both sides with the white pearls of the streetlights.

Mom took a deep breath as if inhaling the beauty of the night. "Did you know Paris is called 'The City of Lights'?" The kids shook their heads, anticipating one of their mom's history lessons. She obliged. "In the 1600s, King Louis the Fourteenth - which the French spell 'L-O-U-I-S' but it's pronounced 'Louie', by the way - placed lanterns on street corners and required his citizens to put candles in their windows to keep the streets safe at night."

She looked down at her children with a tired smile. "I'm so proud of you guys. For trusting your instincts and speaking up for what you felt was right. You let your own light shine tonight."

"Even if it was fiscally inconvenient," Mr. Doemner smiled as he put his arm around Mrs. Doemner.

"What do you say we head back to the hotel and have a hot 'tubby' before bed?" she suggested.

Cora scoffed: "Pfft... Mom. We have no time for bubble baths. We are NOT going to bed until this case is solved. We need to get back into that kitchen right now and look for clues before someone messes up our crime scene!"

Mr. Doemner raised his eyebrows. "Crime scene, huh? Since when did you become a full-fledged detective?"

"Since I read about a hundred Nancy Drew novels," she smirked.

"Fair enough," her dad responded. "So, *Mademoiselle* Detective, what's our next move?"

Cora hesitated, rubbing the back of one calf with the top of her black combat boot. "Well... We need to look at the kitchen and interrogate the staff."

Jackson chimed in: "Follow the trail of the truffles."

"Like pigs!" Mrs. Doemner giggled. Jackson looked confused... and a little insulted.

"They use pigs to find truffles," his mom explained. "The pigs sniff around, then dig up the dirt to unearth the truffles."

Bradley jumped on the idea with relish. "Yes!" he shouted, pumping his fist. "We are Pig Detectives, digging up the dirt to unearth the Bad Guys! Muahahaha!" he threw back his head and laughed like a maniacal villain. Encouraged by everyone's laughter, he started snorting.

Cora shook her head. Bradley always had a unique way of seeing things. She waited until he finished. "Yeah okay, so first we'll talk to the staff. Who would want to steal the truffles? How did they do it? And we need to keep our eyes out for clues."

"What kind of clues?" Jackson asked with a yawn.

Mrs. Doemner squinted at him, and looked at her phone to check the time: After 8 o'clock. "Alright, Cora, we can investigate for one hour, ok? Then we need to get everyone into bed," she said.

There were general grumbles as their dad shepherded them all back into the kitchen. "Shall we start with Monsieur Bocuse?"

. . .

Monsieur Bocuse was not in his office, but his wife Doreen was.

The office looked more like a closet with a window facing the kitchen. Madame Doreen sat behind a metal desk, glancing at receipts and typing into her computer. She was the complete opposite of her husband. While Monsieur Bocuse was tall, she was short. He was jolly and round, she was sharp and thin. His face invariably wore a smile, but her mouth turned down at the corners.

His eyes crinkled, but Doreen's forehead creased. Cora thought they looked like a grape and raisin.

All the Doemners squished inside the small office and carefully closed the door for privacy.

Looking up, Madame Doreen exclaimed, "Ah, Madame Doemner, I'm so glad you're here, so I can thank you also for your generosity!"

She got up, tugged down her black dress suit, and adjusted the polka dot scarf tied around her neck. She came around the desk to give Mr. and Mrs. Doemner the requisite *bises* on each cheek. She looked down at the children and her face pinched into a tight smile.

"And so good to meet you all." She leaned down towards Cora and said in an unnaturally high voice: "You were in your *Maman*'s tummy when we saw you last."

Cora pressed her lips together into a polite-looking smile. She wasn't sure what to say to someone who'd known her as a fetus.

Madame Doreen slid herself back into her chair on the other side of the desk, and motioned for them to sit down in the two wooden chairs before her.

The boys sat down and she asked, "*Puis-je vous aider?* How can I help you?"

Cora looked at her dad, but he nudged his head towards Madame Doreen, silently urging her: *Go on.*

Cora swallowed and opened her sketchbook. Choosing the sharpest pencil she could find, she started, "Madame Bocuse? We are investigating the disappearance of the truffles. Would you mind telling us about the truffles?" She cleared her throat. "Where did they come from? Who might have had access to them? That sort of thing." Cora exhaled. She had thought her parents were going to handle this stuff. She had envisioned herself studying the red tile floor with a magnifying glass, wearing a plaid deerstalker hat like Sherlock Holmes, not talking to annoyed-looking adults. She mentally scribbled a caricature of Madame Bocuse, with her plastered smile fake and exaggerated.

"Of course," Madame Doreen responded curtly. She reached down, pulling out a deep drawer filled with files. She rifled through them and pulled out a yellow sheet of paper with pale blue printing and a dark blue scrawl at the bottom. "Last week Auguste ordered our annual shipment of white truffles from our vendor in Alba, Italy."

She held out the paper to Mr. Doemner. "Here is the receipt from this morning's delivery. It looks like Chef Pierre — Monsieur Broulliet," she clarified. "Received the shipment at 6:23 in the morning. Auguste had a migraine this morning, so he and I came into the restaurant late today. About 3:30, so we could help prepare for dinner."

Mr. Doemner glanced at the sheet before handing it to Cora. Jackson and Bradley poked their heads over her shoulders to read it, too. They couldn't understand much, because it was in French, but they saw the timestamp and a scrawly P — B — - in the signature line.

Cora quickly took notes:

6:23 am
M. B. Migraine
Bocuses arrived late - 3:30pm

"When were the truffles discovered missing?" Jackson asked.

"Evidently, an hour or so ago… Whenever Chef Pierre called the police."

"And you never saw them? The truffles?" Cora pressed.

"*Non*," Madame Doreen answered. "Auguste was busy in the front of the house, getting ready for customers. I have been here in the office, working on finances. Chef Pierre is our Head of Cuisine; he is in charge of all food preparation." Her fake smile had disappeared, replaced with a look of challenge. Madame Bocuse looked annoyed, as if Cora were wasting her time.

Cora snapped a photo of the yellow receipt on her phone and handed it back to Madame Doreen. She consulted her notes in her book. "Well, all roads lead to Chef Pierre. May we talk to him?"

Madame Doreen sucked in her breath through pursed lips and vaguely shook her head. "I don't see how that will be possible. It's only Tuesday night, but this is our busiest time," she said, looking at the clock.

"But it's almost bedtime!" Bradley exclaimed.

Madame Doreen's lips curled in a derisive smile: "Not in Par-EE!"

"The French pronounce Paris 'Par-EE'," Jackson whispered to Bradley, after he noticed the confusion on his face.

"Families are just now coming in to start eating, and usually dinner takes at least two hours," Mr. Doemner informed him.

Bradley's mouth dropped open, then slowly curved into a mischievous grin. "You hear that, Mom?" He looked up at her. "No bed till eleven!" he crowed.

She laughed. "Too bad you're American, my love. I still want you in bed by nine."

Bradley pouted and Jackson groaned. Cora, ignoring her brothers, looked at Madame Doreen with eyes squinted. "Just five minutes?" she pleaded.

Madame Doreen paused, then finally nodded and stood up. "Alright, *cinq minutes*," and she squeezed past to lead them into the kitchen. Cora's pulse got faster, and she thought she could hear her heartbeat from outside of her body.

Chef Pierre Broulliet was the short, angry chef who had been accusing Jeanne earlier. As they entered the kitchen, he yelled at the staff: "*Vite, vite, vite!*" Everyone seemed to be rushing. They were quickly chopping vegetables, quickly stirring sauces, quickly piping whipped cream into puff pastries, carrying full dishes trailing delicious-smelling steam into the dining room, and carrying empty dishes from the dining room to be washed in the sink. Everyone moved as fast as they could, and Chef Pierre stood in the center, directing traffic like a cop.

Madame Doreen called him over, and Chef Pierre glared at the Doemners as he came. Bullets shot from his eyes.

"*Oui?*" he asked Madame Doreen, arms crossed.

"I have explained to the Doemners how busy we are at dinner time, but they would like to ask you a few questions about the truffles." Then Madame Doreen bowed slightly to excuse herself and returned to the office.

Chef Pierre raised one eyebrow and his lips became a tight, thin line, perfectly matching the mustache on his top lip. Refusing to acknowledge the children or Mrs. Doemner, he scowled at Mr. Doemner and practically barked - "*Oui*?"

Mr. Doemner placed his hand on Cora's shoulder and she gulped. Back home, her neighbors had a gray French bulldog named Buck who barked whenever they rang the doorbell. Buck had bitten her finger once when she tried to pet him. She felt like she was facing Buck now. This French man was not much taller than herself, but he clearly wanted to growl at her. *He's already proven he can bite*, she thought, thinking of poor Jeanne in handcuffs.

She told herself that sometimes small animals made themselves large and loud to scare you because they felt scared themselves. She took a deep breath, clutching her open sketchbook in the crook of her arm. Her pencil hovered over the page at the ready. "*Monsieur* Broulliet," she said in her most respectful tone. "We understand you collected the truffles at 6:23 this morning. Could you tell us what happened to them?"

Chef Pierre frowned. He did not expect to be addressed by this girl-child who had invaded his kitchen. He looked from Mr. Doemner, down to Cora, and then back to Mr. Doemner in disgust. His brow furrowed and he directed his answer at Mr. Doemner: "After I received zee truffles, we packed zem into a glass jar with arborio rice, sealed de lid, and placed zem in zee crisper." He pointed towards the large refrigerator that had been standing open earlier.

Cora felt her head fill with hot steam. *He's ignoring me on purpose!* she realised. She took a deep breath to ask another question when Bradley interrupted: "How did you fit four thousand mushrooms into a jar of rice?" he asked.

Chef Pierre looked confused and said to Bradley: "*Quatre mille* mushrooms?" He looked back at Mr. Doemner again for clarification.

Mr. Doemner explained, "No Bradley, it was four thousand *euros*,

not four thousand truffles. They said it was a little over a pound...
I'm not sure how many truffles that would be...?" he looked at
Chef Pierre, holding his hands out to about the size of a cantaloupe
melon as a question.

"Ah, no," the Chef sneered at Bradley's misunderstanding with
a mocking cackle, "Only eight truffles. And zey vere beauties!"

The arrogant man looked back at the refrigerator with a sigh as if
he had sealed his lover in the jar with the rice. "And zen... gone!"
The wistfulness reverted to rage. "We had zem for lunch — our
white truffle pasta with prawns. *c'est très magnifique* — and zen
when I opened zee crisper to start tonight's risotto, zee entire jar
was missing!" His eyes flashed, as if he blamed the Doemners for
the truffles' absence.

Cora broke through his flames of anger: "So why did you think
it was Jeanne?"

Pierre slowly slid his steely stare off Mr. Doemner and locked
eyes with Cora. "BECAUSE."

Cora felt a heavy black weight pressing into her chest as he leaned
closer and said quietly: "Zat—" he spit out a word that could only
be an insult "was the only one here between lunch and dinner." He
stepped back and looked at Mr. Doemner, whose nostrils were flared.
"So you see — zere is no case. The truffles vere here for lunch.
Everyone went on break except zee dirty dishwasher, and when
we returned to start dinner, zey vere gone." He sneered. "But you
have paid off my boss and let a thief go free, so what's to be done?"

And with that, he turned and started issuing orders again, this
time with a smirk crinkling one corner of his mouth.

5

CHAPTER CINQ

GOTTA KEEP IT COOL

Cora wanted to roar at the Chef as he walked away. Instead, she slammed her sketchbook shut, spun on her heel, and marched her family over to the crisper. Piles of fruits and vegetables filled the huge walk-in refrigerator with as many colors as the gems in the King's Crown. Every shelf was packed with produce, except the middle shelf where a large glass jar of rice-packed truffles should have been standing.

Cora leaned over to examine the floor, her nose just inches from the tile.

"What are you looking for?" her mom asked.

"Clues," Cora responded, although truthfully, she didn't really know.

"Like what?"

Cora shrugged. "I won't know until I see them, will I?"

Mr. and Mrs. Doemner exchanged glances. Her family knew not to get in her way when she was on the warpath.

Her brothers stood and stared around at the shelves, obviously unimpressed. Jackson shivered and rubbed his bare arms. "I'm gonna go stand outside."

"Me too," Bradley agreed, and they stepped back into the warm kitchen. Mrs. Doemner followed.

Cora jumped, startled, when the door clicked shut behind them. Mr. Doemner chuckled. "Don't worry, it's not a horror film, honey. See that handle there?" He pointed at a large metal lever on the door. "We can push that to walk out any time. And the light should stay on as long as we're moving." He waved at the lightbulb in the ceiling.

Cora shook off the goosebumps, telling herself it was just the cold air, and kept searching for clues. Unfortunately, there were only a few scuff marks on the floor — no clearly visible footprints that would identify the thief's shoe size and sole pattern. *Bummer*. And dusting for fingerprints would be useless because everyone came in here to grab what they needed for their recipes. If only the thief had caught their robe on a protruding nail and left a small section of cloth that fit perfectly to a hole in their sleeve... She started daydreaming of how easy this crime would be to solve if only she really were Nancy Drew.

She almost hit her head on a shelf in alarm when the door swung open suddenly to reveal a tall young man with blond hair, wearing a floppy white chef's hat. He seemed just as surprised to find two Americans hiding in his cooler as Cora by his abrupt appearance. Cora remembered him as the chef who had comforted Jeanne.

"*Bonjour*," Mr. Doemner said, extending his hand.

The chef hesitantly replied *"Bonjour?"* as he shook Mr. Doemner's hand.

"Zhur muh pell Cora," Cora said, holding her hand out to be shaken as well.

The chef smiled at the sight of the American girl in the crisper, took her hand, and bowed over as if to kiss it, but stopped with his lips hovering only an inch above. *"Enchanté, Mademoiselle* Cora," he said with a playful grin. He stood up. *"Je m'appelle,* Leo," he said, placing his hand on his heart.

Cora blushed to the tips of her red hot ears. No one had ever tried to kiss her hand before. Like she was a princess. Mr. Doemner bit his lip to swallow a guffaw. "Perhaps you'd like to ask Leo a few questions?" he suggested, grinning through his thick beard.

Cora looked into Leo's blue eyes. Her mind went strangely blank. "Uhh…"

Mr. Doemner came to her rescue: "What do you do here, Leo?"

"Je suis l'entremétier," he said to Mr. Doemner. "I am the Vegetable and Sauces Chef," he explained to Cora. "I work with our produce vendors to get the freshest fruits and vegetables and

then prepare them for use in the recipes. Lots and lots of chopping and sauteing," he laughed.

Again, Mr, Deomner waited for Cora to chime in. She studied her toes.

"Your English is excellent," her dad observed at last.

"Ah, *merci* — Thank you! I went to school in the States." He turned and grabbed several carrots, a stalk of celery, and two brown onions. "When I got back, my uncle connected me to Monsieur Bocuse, and *voila*!" he smiled, standing up straight, arms full of vegetables.

Mr. Doemner nudged Cora and whispered, "Truffles?"

She looked at him and blinked. *Oh yeah… Jeanne!* She shook her head, feeling like an idiot and blurted out as Leo prepared to leave the crisper: "Did you see the truffles when they came in this morning?"

Leo turned, hands full, and nodded. "Yes, Chef Pierre left them on my station, asking me to brush and pack them into the rice jar. I set it there when I was done." He nodded towards the conspicuously empty shelf.

Cora's eyes grew big. Chef Pierre had said *he* had packed up the truffles, but it had been Leo! "When did you see the truffles last?" she asked..

Leo paused, looking up at the corner of the crisper. "Let's see.. We were shaving one throughout lunch. I tossed it back in the rice around 2:30, I think... Just before I left on break."

"And they weren't there when you got back?"

"Well," Leo twisted his mouth as he thought. "I didn't go looking for them until about 5:30 when the first order for risotto came through. That's when I noticed they were gone and informed Chef Pierre."

Cora pulled herself together enough to scratch into her book:

Leo discovered they were missing.

"And what about Jeanne? Did you see her anywhere near the truffles?"

Leo's face darkened, and it looked as if his mind sailed far away. "No. Poor girl. She had her hands full with dishes at the sink. She was still washing up from lunch when I got back from my break."

"When was that?" Cora inquired.

He bit his lip. "Around four, I would say? I could check my time stamp — we all have to clock in and out when we leave."

Cora nodded, mind racing, wondering what else she should ask him.

Leo turned to leave, but stopped. "Perhaps I am overstepping…" he hesitated. Cora encouraged him to go on. "…but I always felt sorry for Jeanne." He sighed. "As you may have noticed, we don't have many women in our kitchen and it was harder for Jeanne because she's…" he paused. "Well… different." A soft smile crossed his lips.

Cora remembered something: "Chef Pierre called her a… " Cora leaned towards Leo and whispered the word. "What does that mean?"

Leo's face grew red. "He said that to you?" he almost shouted. His fingers gripped the vegetables so tightly his knuckles turned white. "That…" he stopped and clenched his jaw. He took a deep breath. "It's a bad word for people from Africa. I can't believe he said that to you." He shook his head. "Well, I guess I should not be too surprised. It makes sense, really. Chef Pierre is not popular with any of us, but he always seems to go out of his way to make Jeanne's life miserable."

He stared vaguely in the direction of the dishwashing station, as if remembering Jeanne standing over in her corner. He looked ready to punch a wall.

"Why is that?" Cora asked.

"Why?" Leo repeated, looking down at her. He sighed. "Unfortunately, there is still a lot of prejudice and racism in my country towards Algerians. France took over Algeria in 1830 and when the Algerians were fighting for their independence, several terrorist attacks in Paris killed many French citizens. Many Parisians have become suspicious of Muslims, I fear."

Cora knew that Muslims were people who believed in the Prophet Muhammed. This explained Jeanne's head covering, because traditionally, Muslim women covered their hair as a sign of modesty and an act of faith.

When she looked up, Leo was watching her with a kind expression.

"By the way," he leaned a little closer to her. "I saw you defending Jeanne. That was very brave."

Cora blushed and looked down at her shoes again.

Leo addressed Mr. Doemner. "And thank you, *Monsieur*, for interceding. That was very generous."

Cora smiled at Mr. Doemner. "So, you don't think Jeanne did it?" she asked Leo.

"*Non!*" Leo's face flashed in anger again. Then he stopped, catching himself. He cleared his throat and proceeded as if it were no big deal. "Jeanne has only been here a few months, but she always worked hard and was kind to everyone. Quiet, but not secretive. I do not think she would have done such a thing," he responded, shaking his head adamantly.

They heard Chef Pierre shouting in the kitchen. Leo grimaced, "*Excusez-moi, Monsieur et Mademoiselle...* I must be getting back." He beamed a bright smile at Cora and walked out of the refrigerator.

Mr. Doemner shivered. "Well, Miss Detective, enough sleuthing for now? Can we go warm up?"

Cora hadn't even noticed the cold, but as they emerged from the crisper and saw Chef Pierre shouting at his team, an icy finger raised the hairs on her neck.

6

CHAPTER SIX

EVERYTHING IS GREEN

Bradley rubbed his eyes and looked around the hotel room. Sunlight slipped through the cracks in their curtains. He rolled over and found his brother, Jackson, still sleeping on the pillow next to him, eyes closed, mouth open. Bradley couldn't resist sticking his finger into Jackson's mouth and poking his tongue.

"Gah!" Jackson spat out the finger. "Brad-leeeee!" he wailed in frustration, and without even opening his eyes, he flopped over to his other side and pulled a second pillow up on top of his head for protection.

"Good morning, Gackson!" Bradley laughed, unconsciously using the nickname he had given Jackson as a baby.

He ran to the window and jerked back the floor-to-ceiling blackout drapes and a flood of sunlight poured into the hotel room. Cora, sleeping in the queen-sized bed next to the boys, groaned and pulled the white sheets up over her face.

They were on the sixth floor of an apartment building with a glorious view of the Eiffel Tower out the window.

"Best Day Ever!" Bradley sang his hallmark phrase with arms wide open. A pillow flew across the room and smacked him in the back of the head. "Co-wah!" he fumed and chucked the pillow back at his sister.

He followed the pillow, running over the carpet to pounce on his sister. "Cora, it's time to wake up!" he said as he bounced up and down on her legs.

A growl emanated from under the sheets, and next thing Bradley knew, he was flat on his back with a Cora on top of him, pinning him down with Tickle-Fingers. He laughed and screamed and cried and squirmed, but Cora refused to stop tickling, until he finally gasped out: "Cora! Stop! We can't waste time, we have work to do!"

Instantly she sat up, eyes wide. "That's right! We have to prove Jeanne's innocence today!"

She hopped out of bed and dragged the pillow off Jackson's head. He writhed when the sun hit his face and tried to burrow back under the covers, but Cora shouted, "Come on, Jackson, you gotta get up! We have to help Jeanne."

Cora ran to the closet, tossing her pajamas into the collapsible hamper Mom always brought on trips, and pulling a knee-length dress over her head. Bradley followed suit, taking a bit longer as he worked to pull the zipper up on his jeans, then out into the living room to help Cora wake up their parents.

Jackson heard Cora shout "Let's go find breakfast!" just before he buried himself back under the pillows.

• • •

"So you guys are really serious about this?" Mr. Doemner asked.

"Yes!" all three Doemner children shouted. They were drinking hot chocolate and eating buttery *croissants* at an outdoor cafe. The chocolate was thick as a melted chocolate bar, and not as sweet as the powdered stuff they drank back home in the States.

Mrs. Doemner had just left to finish up her work at the Petit Palais. Mr. Doemner had hoped a good night's sleep might dissuade them from their detective ambitions. Cora, however, refused to be deterred; she was determined to solve the case.

Mr. Doemner relented, realizing he would have to adjust their touristy plans. "Alright, so what's next? And what are we doing exactly?"

Bradley looked at Jackson. Jackson looked at Cora. Cora looked at her ring. Realizing she would have to start with the accused, she offered, "I think we should go talk to Jeanne. We didn't get a chance to ask her who SHE thought the culprit was."

"Seems reasonable," Mr. Doemner agreed.

"Did your ring tell you that?" Jackson asked sarcastically. Cora did not bother answering him; he could doubt if he wanted.

Mr. Doemner pulled up the map, entered the address from Cora's sketchbook and found her house on the other side of the Seine river, near Montmartre. He called Jeanne to confirm they could visit, and they headed across town via the Métro.

Dad insisted they see the Sacré-Cœur Basilica first, so after a short delay for a ride around the carousel and "about 10,000 stairs," the family finally reached the brilliantly white Basilica.

"Montmartre is the tallest hill in Paris," Mr. Doemner said as he spread his arms, showing them the whole city below them. "'Montmartre' means 'Mountain of the Martyrs'. The most famous martyr, Saint Denis, the first bishop of Paris, was beheaded right here on this hill."

Cora wrinkled her nose in disgust but the boys eagerly looked around, as if searching for a body.

Her father continued, "But what's even crazier is that after Saint Denis was beheaded, they say he picked up his own head and gave a sermon. He walked down the hill, all the way to the river, where he finally gave up the ghost. Literally."

All three of their mouths dropped open. "That's crazy!" Jackson said as he envisioned the horrific sight.

"Did that really happen?" Cora asked, her voice tinged with awe.

Mr. Doemner shrugged. "That's what historians said. Now, this was back in, like, 270 A.D when the Roman empire still ruled the city, so we don't have any way to verify it, but it makes a good story, doesn't it? Saint Denis was the first talking head," he added, laughing at his own joke.

"What's that?" Bradley pointed backwards towards the Basilica, up at two horse sculptures perched above the three curved arches.

Mr. Doemner consulted his guide book. "The one on the left is Saint Louis, a King of France in the Middle Ages and namesake of a famous city in Missouri. And the one on the right is your favorite heroine, Cora — Joan of Arc."

"Jeanne d'Arc," Cora corrected him, impressed with herself now that she knew the correct French way to pronounce it. She loved the feel of the words on her tongue.

"Why are they green?" Jackson asked.

"They're made of metal. It's called a 'patina' - it's what happens to copper when it's exposed to water and air. You see that same effect on another famous French statue - our Statue of Liberty!"

Cora raised an eyebrow. "The Statue of Liberty is French? She's, like, the symbol of America!"

Mr. Doemner laughed. "Yes, now she is. But the French gave her to us 100 years after we won the Revolutionary War. In fact, the same man who built the Eiffel Tower here in Paris," he pointed out to the horizon where you could see the Tower even taller than where they now stood on the hill, "his name was Alexandre-Gustave Eiffel — he designed the inside of the Statue of Liberty for the sculptor who covered her in copper skin."

Just then, bells began ringing, with sound waves that jarred their bodies. Bradley covered his ears, but Jackson closed his eyes as if meditating.

Cora started tugging on her dad's sleeve."Come on, Dad! We're going to waste the whole day if we don't get to Jeanne's soon!"

"Okay, let's take a quick selfie." He huddled them together, with Bradley grinning so hard it looked like a grimace and Jackson holding up "bunny ears" behind Cora's head in the photo.

Finally, Cora managed to drag them all down the other side of the hill to Jeanne's apartment complex. It was the same six-story, limestone building that the kids felt they had seen everywhere else in Paris.

They buzzed her via intercom and the kids heard a loud click as she unlocked the gate remotely from her room. They climbed three flights of stairs, and were soon knocking on her door.

"Bonjour, *mes amis*! Hello, my friends!" Jeanne welcomed them into the apartment.

Jackson was not sure what he had expected, but certainly his ideas had been a lot more exotic than what he saw. They walked past a small kitchen on the left into a living room with a window on the far side. Two plaid couches faced a flat-screen television and an older boy with dark skin and eyes like Jeanne's, turned off the show he'd been watching and walked over.

"This is my brother, Sami," Jeanne introduced him. He shook their hands.

"Enchantée," Cora said, proud of her French.

"Enchanté," Sami returned with a smile.

He chatted in French to his sister, then kissed her cheek, waved goodbye, and exited the front door.

Jeanne explained, "He's off to work, but was very happy to meet you." She smiled and motioned towards the couches. "Won't you come in? Can I get you some tea?"

Jackson shook his head, but Mr. Doemner quickly said, "Yes, that would be lovely, thank you," and he shepherded them towards the couches, while Jeanne moved to the kitchen.

"Jeanne's family is from northern Africa," he whispered in explanation. "Serving tea is a sign of hospitality for many cultures. Make sure you try at least a little bit, okay?" he said, looking in particular at Bradley, who had a tendency to be very honest about what he liked and did not like to eat. All three kids nodded.

Just then, a tall woman with light skin and blue eyes, wearing a red hijab headscarf just like Jeanne's purple one, walked in the front door with a large cloth bag in her arms. Peeking out of the top of the bag, the Doemners could see the bushy tops of carrots and the golden dome of a freshly-baked *baguette*.

She paused when she saw them in her living room, and they heard Jeanne's voice from the kitchen. "These are my friends, *Maman*, the Doemners. The ones who came to my aid last night."

The woman's face instantly passed from hesitant curiosity into a wide grin as if she had known the family for years. She hurriedly set down her groceries and rushed over to the family, shaking hands and kissing all of them on both cheeks, except Mr. Doemner who she stood a few feet away from but still showered him with a look of pure joy. Jackson rubbed his cheeks off, but Bradley loved the attention.

"Oh, *merci beaucoup!*" she said to them all. "I cannot thank you enough for helping our Jeanne."

Jeanne came into the living room carrying a large tray with a tall, ornately decorated silver tea pot and six short, delicate cups made of glass.

"Jeanne told us about the confusion at the restaurant and we are so grateful you stepped in," Madame Mokhtari continued in flawless English with only a hint of a French accent.

"It was the right thing to do," Mr. Doemner replied. "I can only hope someone would have done the same for my daughter in the same circumstances." He placed a hand on Cora's head next to him and smiled down at her. At that moment, Mr. Doemner realized that following his daughter's insistence to work on this case had been the right decision.

Jeanne carefully placed the tray on the low table sitting between the couches and gestured for her mother to take the tea pot. Madame Mokhtari grabbed the handle and began to pour tea into a glass, starting low, then increasingly higher, until the steaming liquid arched almost three feet before splashing into the glass. The kids were enthralled. Madame Mokhtari continued the same spectacular pouring technique for the remaining five glasses, never spilling a drop.

When she finished, Mr. Doemner clapped and the kids joined in. "Wow!" Bradley exclaimed. "That was awesome!"

She smiled and handed each of them a frothy cup of tea.

"Is that how they pour tea in France?" Bradley asked.

Madame Mokhtari chuckled. "*Non*; it is how I pour tea in France. It is an Algerian custom. I learned it when I married my husband."

Bradley looked around. "Where is he?"

Madame Mokhtari looked down and swallowed before answering with a sad smile, "I'm afraid he passed away when the kids were younger. That's when we moved back here, where I'm from."

Cora instinctively reached out to hug the elegant lady who suddenly seemed very fragile. Madame Mokhtari choked out a sound from her gut, a cross between a laugh and a sob, and hugged her back.

Jackson wrapped his hands around the warm cup and sniffed the amber liquid. "Is it mint?" he asked.

Jeanne smiled. "Good nose, Jackson! It's green tea with fresh mint leaves."

Bradley had just taken his first, cautious taste. "And sugar!" he exclaimed in delight, taking another slurpy sip.

"Yes, and lots of sugar, just for you Bradley," Jeanne laughed. Bradley blushed.

Also on the tray were a plate of macarons — pink cookies sandwiching strawberry jam, pale cookies with chocolate ganache, and... "Green cookies?" Bradley held up the grass-colored confection.

"*Oui*," Jeanne nodded. "They are pistachio. My personal favorite."

Bradley again took a hesitant nibble. "MMMM!!" he enthusiastically approved and shoved the rest of the cookie into his mouth. "Der dewicious," he mumbled, with crumbs escaping as he talked.

Mr. Doemner shook his head and handed him a napkin. "Finish chewing before you talk, Dude."

Cora had just finished a pink macaron, and confirmed, "These really are delicious, Jeanne. Where did you get them? We'll need to get some for Mom!"

Jeanne blushed and Madame Mokhtari said, "Jeanne made them herself. She loves to bake. She wanted to be a pastry chef. That's why she was working at the restaurant." She had sat beside Jeanne on the shorter sofa, and placed her hand on Jeanne's shoulder. Jeanne looked down at her tea.

"Right," Jackson said, setting his empty tea cup down on the table. He put on his serious face and got to business. "That's why we're here. We need to prove you're innocent so that you can go back to work."

CHAPTER SEPT

TO CATCH A THIEF

"WHAT?!" Madame Mokhtari looked first at Jackson, then at Jeanne. The air had been forced out of her, and she looked at her daughter with shock. "You want to go back to that... place?"

Jeanne immediately put her concern for herself aside and went to sit by her mom. No matter how much she wanted her mother to feel better, Jeanne couldn't see another option. "After what happened, it will be impossible to get a job anywhere else. I have no references. It was my first job."

Madame Mokhtari clucked her tongue and shook her head at the idea of her daughter working at a place that had subjected her to hatred and bigotry, accused her of stealing, and threatened to have her arrested.

Cora agreed with Madame Mokhtari. She wouldn't want to return to that place if Chef Pierre continued to work there. Regardless, whether or not Jeanne wanted to return, Cora still knew they had to clear her name.

Cora opened her sketch book and got a pencil ready to record, "We wanted to ask, who do YOU think stole the truffles?"

Jeanne blinked several times, scanning her memories of every moment in the restaurant. She came up blank, "I have no idea!"

Then she paused again, considering. "I've been thinking over it... honestly, I hoped that maybe no one had stolen the truffles, they had just been misplaced or something."

She frowned. "I hate to think anyone else on staff could have done it. Especially since they watched me get arrested. I cannot think of anyone that evil." She shook her head, as if she could wish the whole situation away.

Cora scoffed and looked at Jackson. He nodded. "Well, we think we have an idea of who did it," she said.

Jeanne looked up. "Oh? *Qui*? Who?"

Cora had planned to keep it a secret, to remain objective while questioning a witness, but Jackson blurted out: "Chef Pierre."

Jeanne's eyes widened. "What makes you say that?"

Cora glared at Jackson but decided to go with it. She was convinced of Jeanne's innocence; they could trust her enough to let her in on their theory.

"First," Cora held out a single finger, "he was the one who received the truffles from the vendor. He's in charge of all the food."

The Doemners looked at Jeanne to see her reaction. She simply nodded.

"Second," Cora continued, holding out two fingers. "He doesn't like you." Jeanne dropped her eyes. Cora felt a pang of guilt for stating this obvious fact, but it was true, so it had to be said.

"And, third… He's mean." Cora stopped, three fingers in the air. Everyone waited. "That's all I have," she finished.

Mr. Doemner cleared his throat. "That's, uh, not much of a case, there, Cora."

Cora objected, "What do you mean? I don't think we need much more than that! Chef Pierre is evil!"

Mr. Doemner was not convinced. He started a lecture on the difference between facts and feelings. One that Cora had heard many times in her twelve years. She held up a hand to stop him and sighed. "I know, I know. Which is why I wanted to come here today and see if you had any clues that might point to Chef Pierre," she said to Jeanne. "Can you help us prove he did it?"

Mr. Doemner wagged a finger back and forth at Cora, "That isn't the question Cora. You have to separate your feelings about Chef Pierre from the investigation. He may be guilty of being a jerk, but that doesn't make him guilty of stealing truffles. You need to remain open to all possibilities if you want to be a good detective."

"Okay, fine." Cora changed her tactic. "Is there anything else you can think of that can help us figure this out?"

Jeanne creased her eyebrows. "Oh, I don't know. I think I have said everything I know. I cannot think of anything more," she paused, staring at the ceiling, deep in thought.

Jackson put his chin in his hands, resting on his knees, staring vaguely in the direction of the tea cup. Cora started chewing on her nail, allowing Jeanne time to think. Mr. Doemner reached out to stop Bradley from stuffing a fourth macaron into his mouth. "Last one," he said, and his son nodded. Bradley started nibbling the chocolate ganache very slowly, in a circle, savoring every crumb.

Mr. Doemner, in an attempt to move the investigation further, asked, "So what DO we know, Cora?"

Cora opened her sketchbook to a page where she had drawn a chart the night before. She had been unable to fall asleep from all the excitement, and sat up in bed until after midnight trying to make sense of her notes.

She read her notes out loud: "6:23am - the truffles arrived. Chef Pierre gave them to Leo, who cleaned them, put them in a jar of rice, which seems kind of crazy, and placed them in the crisper."

"The rice keeps the truffles dry. The rice also tastes like truffles when we use it to make risotto," Jeanne explained.

Cora cocked her head to the side and scribbled something in her book. "That makes sense I guess." She continued reading, "They used one truffle at lunch and returned it to the aforementioned jar of rice. Chef Pierre said that everyone went on break except you, Jeanne, and their timecards seem to confirm that."

She showed them all the table she had made, noting everyone's break times:

Name	Time In	Time Out	Time In	Time Out
Leo Nowak	11:01 am	2:33 pm	3:54 pm	
Pierre Brouillat	6:15 am	2:45 pm	3:36 pm	
Auguste Bocuse			3:23 pm	
Jeanne Mokhtari	12:24 pm			7:52 pm

"Leo said the truffles were in the crisper when he left for break and they weren't there when he went to grab them for dinner, around 5:30," she added. "So, Jeanne, did you notice anything… unusual?"

Jeanne sat back on the sofa and looked at the ceiling again, gently biting her bottom lip. "No," she gently shook her head. Cora suppressed a wave of frustration, but remained silent hoping that Jeanne might land on something new if she didn't push her.

They all waited, the silence increasingly awkward. Finally, Jeanne's expression lit up. Looking at Cora, she said, "Well, actually… Chef Pierre did send me back into the dining room to do one last sweep for dishes, to make sure the bus boys did not miss anything. It's not terribly unusual, but when I got back, he was gone."

"Ah ha!" Cora shouted. "That's it! That's when he went in and stole the truffles!"

"Uh, Cora," Jackson spoke up. "Jeanne NOT seeing Chef Pierre take the truffles, does not prove that Chef Pierre stole the truffles. I'm with Dad. Innocent until proven guilty, right?"

Cora glared at Jackson. "I know *that*, but that's clearly when he stole them. I am sure of it. All we are missing here is the proof!"

"ALL?!" Jackson scoffed. "That's like… everything. You are missing everything, Cora."

Although Cora didn't want to admit it, he was right. Everyone in the room retreated into their own heads, thinking about the problem. Except Bradley, who got restless and wandered over to the window to stare outside.

"I still don't understand why anyone would want to steal stinky old mushrooms." he said as he looked outside.

"Because they're worth four thousand Euros, of course!" Cora exclaimed.

"Who would pay four thousand dollars for mushrooms?" he asked in disbelief.

"Euros," Mr. Doemner muttered into his tea.

Cora began to turn red and took a deep breath, preparing to argue with her little brother when Jackson held up a hand. She stopped, chest inflated, words unspoken.

"He's right," Jackson said.

"He didn't even say anything. And everything he *did* say was wrong!"

"I mean, he's asking the right question: Who WOULD pay for truffles?"

"You mean, what would Chef Pierre have done with the truffles after he stole them?" Madame Mokhtari asked.

"Exactly," Jackson nodded.

Cora was floored. Once again, she had underestimated her younger brother. Perhaps she had underestimated both of them actually. Bradley had helped without realizing he was even helping. She wrote in her book, "What would be the motivation for someone to steal the truffles? WHY?"

Mr. Doemner stroked his beard while Cora absent-mindedly squiggled random doodles decorating the question 'WHY?'. That question hung heavy in the air.

Bradley, still looking out the window, said, "Why are all the cars in France so tiny? They look like toys!"

Jackson held out a hand to Bradley. "There he goes again! Brilliant, Bradley."

Cora looked at her brother like he'd lost his mind. Bradley was many things. Brazen maybe. Bold. Definitely boisterous. But brilliant?

"His CAR," Jackson explained. "Chef Pierre would have taken the truffles to his car, so he could transport them to wherever he was going!"

Cora jumped up. "That's it! If we can find some sign of the truffles in his car — maybe some grains of rice in his trunk — then we've got him!" Her blue eyes shone behind her turquoise glasses, her fist outstretched like she was grabbing Chef Pierre's wrist in triumph.

"Maybe he hasn't even had a chance to sell them yet, and they're still in his car!" Jackson suggested. "Then we could get your money back, Dad!"

Mr. Doemner grinned and said, "That would be lovely, but let's not count our chickens before they hatch. Let's head back to the restaurant and see what we can find." He stood. "Jeanne, do you happen to know which car is Chef Pierre's?"

She nodded and rose. "*Oui*, I will come with you." With that, she bent down to kiss her *Maman* on the cheek and walked into the back rooms to get ready.

Madame Mokhtari, still looking concerned for her daughter, stood and walked the Doemners to the front door. She shook Mr. Doemner's hand. "*Merci encore*," she said. "Thank you again. Our family is in your debt, for all that you have done and are trying to do for Jeanne. Please, watch out for her if you return to the restaurant? I would like to not worry so much while she is gone."

Cora looked at her dad and observed an expression she rarely saw on her dad's face. His eyes were teary. He looked down at Cora and pulled her into an embrace. "Madame, you have my promise. I will watch out for her as I would for my own daughter."

Tears of gratitude poured down Madame Makhtari's cheeks and Mr. Doemner started to blush when Bradley asked loudly, "Can we take these home?" pointing at the remaining macarons.

Madame Mokhtari wiped her face with the back of her hand and smiled saying, "*Bien sûr!* Of course!" At the exact moment, Jeanne re-entered the room and she said, "Wait! I have something better."

Going into the kitchen, she brought out a pretty metal tin from the kitchen, already filled with all three kinds of cookies. "*Voila!*" she said, handing the tin carefully to Bradley.

Holding his new prized possession carefully, he exclaimed, "Mer-see!" Everyone chuckled at the little American boy's valiant attempt to speak French. They tucked Bradley's tin of cookies in a bag, said "*Adieu*" to Madame Mokhtari, and followed Jeanne out of the apartment and towards the Métro Station.

They walked up the stairs from the train, blinking in as the bright sunlight fell on the grey limestone of the Notre-Dame Cathedral.

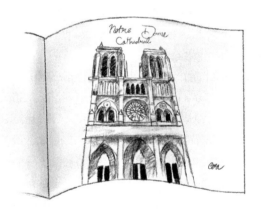

Mr. Doemner walked to the edge of the street, overlooking the River Seine. He pointed toward the twin towers. "Do you guys remember the Disney movie, 'The Hunchback of Notre Dame'? That was set at that church right there. Victor Hugo wrote the book specifically to save Notre-Dame Cathedral. Isn't that cool? A novel saved *that* church."

Jeanne seemed interested in hearing more, but Cora was ready to move on. "Okay, Dad, that's great, but we have a mystery to solve!" She dragged him by the arm down the street.

Small kiosks lined the sidewalk with street vendors selling paintings, souvenirs, and snacks. The linden trees swayed gently in the breeze between them and the river.

Jeanne pointed out a little café: "That is the 'Shakespeare and Company' bookstore - you know it?" she asked Mr. Doemner.

"No, what is it?"

"Its namesake was founded by an American woman, Sylvia Plath. It attracted many English-writers, including Ernest Hemingway, T.S. Elliott, and James Joyce."

That was enough for Mr. Doemner. As a book-lover and history-buff, the idea of a historic bookstore sounded better than candy to him! As if tugged by a rope tied to his waist, he started to cross the street immediately.

"DAD!" Cora ran and clung onto his arm again. "We can go book shopping AFTER we do what we came here to do. Come on!" and she dragged a very reluctant Mr. Doemner closer to Chez Bocuse, the scene of the crime.

At last they arrived and walked past the bright red awnings stretched over the front windows, down the side alley to the small parking lot in the back.

"Okay," Cora said to Jeanne, gesturing towards the cars. "Which one is Chef Pierre's?"

After scanning the rows of cars, Jeanne pointed towards a little red Peugeot in the back corner.

Jackson glanced nervously towards the back entrance of the restaurant, expecting Chef Pierre to come storming through. Jeanne put her hand on his shoulder, "It should be okay. They're all busy with lunch right now." Jeanne's smile made him feel a little more courageous.

"Besides," Cora interjected. "We're not doing anything bad. Just peeking in the windows."

Cora peered into the driver's seat window. Bradley started jumping up and down next to her, trying to see in as well. Mr. Doemner lifted him up. "Don't touch," he warned the squirmy little boy. "We don't want to accidentally set off an alarm."

Bradley conscientiously kept his hands a half inch away from the glass as he formed them into binoculars.

"See anything, buddy?" his dad asked, straining to keep him up at hip-level.

"Trash," Bradley replied, "lots of it. Chef Pierre is gross. Cora, write that in your clue book."

Cora ignored her brother, and her dad asked, "How about you, Cora?"

She didn't answer. She felt frustrated. All she could see were cigarette butts in the center console and miscellaneous papers on the passenger seat. Food wrappers and empty Diet Coke cans were strewn across the back. Any clues would be nearly impossible to spot in a trash heap like this. She reminded herself that a thief probably wouldn't have left a jar of rice conspicuously in plain sight.

"How can we get into his trunk?" she demanded.

"Why do you want to get into his trunk?" a strange male voice asked them from behind.

8

CHAPTER HUIT

Napoleon

RESCUED BY NAPOLEON BONAPARTE

Everyone jumped. Bradley squealed in surprise and Mr. Doemner almost dropped him, catching him by his elbow as he slid back to the pavement. They turned to find a short man in an old-fashioned military uniform, topped with a strange tall black hat folded in on itself like a taco.

Mr. Doemner blinked in disbelief. "Napoleon?"

"At your service," the small man whisked off his hat and bowed elegantly. Bradley returned the dramatic bow, waving his hand in a circle several times before sweeping it and his head down towards the ground.

Confused at this bizarre sight, and also slightly embarrassed, Cora asked, "Who?!"

"Napoleon Bonaparte was a Corsican general who crowned himself Emperor of France after the French Revolution… and he's one of my favorite military heroes," her dad explained as he reached out to shake the man's hand.

"Uh, okay… but who is he *really*?" Cora questioned.

Jeanne leaned over to whisper in Cora's ear: "He is a street performer. People pay to take pictures with him."

Cora raised her eyebrows in surprise, but nodded. Indeed, the man looked like he had just exited a stage, complete with cakey stage makeup and a glistening sheen of sweat dripping onto his collar. He wore a bright blue coat, so short in the front that Cora could see his pot belly protruding from the white chemise underneath, but the back hung down in two long tails that almost dragged on the ground behind him. His bony knees were covered in thick white stockings under short knickers just like children in old pictures used to wear.

"Is this real?" Bradley asked, pointing at the man's long sword.

"Indeed," Napoleon replied, pulling the saber from its scabbard and holding it up, as if ready to charge.

"May we take a picture?" Mr. Doemner asked, handing him several Euros.

"Of course," the man agreed gleefully, standing back and extending his arms to welcome the kids closer.

Mr. Doemner pulled out his phone. "Say cheese," he said. "Or rather, *fromage*!" He chuckled and snapped a photo of his children.

Jeanne, infected by Mr. Doemner's enthusiasm, said to him, "Did you know that photography was invented here in France? Louis Daguerre sold his invention to France, who declared photography a 'gift from France to the world' in 1839."

Cora didn't think her dad's grin could get any bigger, but it did, all his teeth framed by his dark beard. "That's amazing, Jeanne! I had no idea! Do you like history?"

"Very much," she smiled and looked down at the ground. "I wanted to work in a museum when I was a girl."

Jackson and Bradley forced their dad to show them the picture. Everyone was smiling, no one was blinking (even though Cora had her eyes on the car next to them) — Success!

"So... Not to be rude," Napoleon said. "But may I ask why you are peering into what is evidently a stranger's car?"

Jackson looked at Mr. Doemner. Mr. Doemner looked at Cora. Cora looked at Jeanne, who looked down at her feet.

Cora took a deep breath and said, "We're trying to solve a mystery."

"A mystery, you say? I do love mysteries! You must CLUE me in." Napoleon winked. Mr. Doemner was the only one who laughed at the joke. Napoleon, pleased with his reaction, took a short bow.

"Well," Cora said slowly, not sure how much to reveal. "Last night, some truffles were discovered missing at our friend's restaurant." She gestured at the cafe behind her. "Jeanne was blamed, so we're trying to find the real culprit and prove she's innocent."

"Ahh," the small French soldier replied. "And you think the thief hid them in this car?"

Cora nodded. "That, or used it to move them somewhere else."

"Hmmm..." Napoleon stroked his chin. "You know, I come back here to eat lunch almost every afternoon." He pointed towards a corner of the parking lot where they saw a half eaten baguette filled with meat and cheese, sitting on a curb. "Yesterday, I ate later than usual. Sitting in my usual spot, enjoying my *crepes*, when I noticed one of the chefs coming out of the backdoor, carrying a large 'to-go' bag. I might not have noticed, except that he started pacing nervously and kept checking his watch. He called someone on his cell phone and a few minutes later, a car pulled into the driveway. The chef handed the driver the bag and the car drove off quickly. Then the chef got into this car here." He stopped, pointing at the red Peugeot.

Cora's jaw dropped. She wanted to hug Napoleon!

"Yes!" she cried. "This is the evidence we need to prove Chef Pierre stole the truffles! Right, Dad?"

Mr. Doemner shrugged and held up his hands. "It doesn't prove it, but it is certainly enough to make Chef Pierre look suspicious. What time did you say this was?" he asked Napoleon.

Napoleon cocked his head to one side and said, "I would say, around 3 o'clock?"

Cora pulled out her sketchbook and quickly turned to the table she made with the timeline of events. "That's it! It's totally him!" Cora crowed as she pointed to the page. "Chef Pierre got off at 2:45pm - it must have been him selling the truffles to his buyer. That way, there wouldn't even be any evidence in his trunk."

Mr. Doemner pursed his lips and turned back to Napoleon. "Would you feel comfortable sharing this information with my friend, Monsieur Bocuse, who owns the restaurant?"

The street performer shook his hands back and forth and stated adamantly. "I am sorry, sir, but I have to earn my living… I am not a detective, like you."

Jeanne leaned towards Cora and whispered, "I think he wants to be paid."

Cora understood. "Oh, well, I'm sure we could make it worth your while, right, Dad?" she looked at her dad and nudged her head in Napoleon's direction.

"Oh, yes!" Mr. Doemner caught on too. "Of course your time is very valuable…" And he pulled out his wallet, handing the small man several more bills.

Napoleon smirked, and then bowed again. "Of course, I can always make time for friends like you — *mes amis, allons-y!* Let's go!"

With that, Napoleon marched into the restaurant, as if he owned the place.

. . .

Monsieur Bocuse did not take the information well. He looked as if he had seen a ghost. He fell into his chair, then slumped even lower.

"You think Chef Pierre did this?" he asked, brow furrowed.

They scrunched into his office again; this time, even more crowded with the addition of Jeanne and Napoleon.

They had received some mighty curious glances from the staff. Seeing the recently-disgraced Jeanne, following the ostentatious Napoleon with three small American children and their dad who looked like a lumberjack, trooping through the kitchen had been quite the show-stopper.

"But Chef Pierre has been with me since we opened. He is practically my partner." Monsieur Bocuse shook his head.

Cora lost even more respect for Monsieur Bocuse. How could he defend such a despicable person? How could he rationalize keeping this guy around?

Mr. Doemner, who looked like he had just sucked a lemon, cleared his throat. "Well, as we mentioned, we didn't see what was in the bag… would it be possible to ask him about the situation and see what he has to say?"

Cora glared at her dad. Now he wanted to give Chef Pierre a

chance? She leaned over and poked him in the ribs, whispering, "What are you doing?"

Mr. Doemner whispered back, "I know he's not nice, Cora. But we still have to speak with everyone to get to the truth. Sometimes we have to deal with difficult people so we can get to the other side of a bad situation. This is Jeanne's bad situation, and if we want to help her we have to speak to Chef Pierre."

Cora felt her stomach churn, but she knew her dad was right. She would have to swallow her feelings to help her new friend.

Monsieur Bocuse squeezed past them to stick his head out the office: "Pierre, *voulez-vous venir ici, s'il vous plaît?"*

Cora knew that "*voulez-vous venir ici*" meant "would you LIKE to come here." Was Monsieur Bocuse afraid of Chef Pierre? Why didn't he just command him to come?

In order to get Chef Pierre's round belly in, Mr. Doemner had to join Monsieur Bocuse on the other side of the desk, holding Bradley in his arms. Jeanne tucked herself in the most remote corner, as far from her accuser as possible. Napoleon Bonaparte perched himself jauntily on the edge of the desk, as if waiting for a play to begin on a stage.

Monsieur Bocuse started, "Pierre, as you know, the Doemners have been researching the missing truffles and this... gentleman... here," he pointed at Napoleon as if apologizing, "has related an interesting story. I would like to hear what you have to say about it." He gestured to Napoleon to tell his story.

Napoleon fixed his hat, took a deep breath and said, "I do not wish to make trouble, but yesterday, sir, I saw you hand a large bag of what seemed to be food to a driver, who drove off quickly. That is all."

Cora seethed. The story now felt vague. She wanted him to add the part about Chef Pierre looking nervous. She also wanted to point out how quick Chef Pierre had been to blame Jeanne...

Anything to get Pierre to confess!

Chef Pierre puffed out his chest and opened his mouth, like he was preparing to shout, but nothing came out. His already-red face grew redder and sweat trickled down his face. He looked at Monsieur Bocuse and then exhaled.

Cora thought he looked like a balloon deflating.

"I did not steal the truffles," he said loudly, looking at Jeanne, as if he still suspected her. "But I did steal," he said more quietly. "I'm sorry, Auguste. *Ma sœur,* my sister, she just lost her job. She is a single mom; my niece and nephew are so young… She asked if I could help her out, so I took some leftovers from the kitchen yesterday. That is what he saw."

He hung his head.

Cora stared at him. *That's it?* He couldn't be telling the truth! Could he? All signs pointed to him! He was probably just lying to protect himself. How could someone so evil do something kind like give food to a struggling sister? This didn't match up. She wrote "*sister, single, lost job*" in her sketchbook.

Monsieur Bocuse looked relieved. "Ah, Pierre, why did you not tell me? You know I would be happy to help out. I would have preferred we buy her groceries with our own money rather than the restaurant's food, but — "

"Yes, I understand," Chef Pierre interjected, nodding quickly. "I would have told you, but you were not in yesterday. I will definitely use personal money from now on. *Désolé.* I'm sorry."

Monsieur Bocuse smiled, and waved Chef Pierre back to work. "*Oui, oui,* it is all good. *Merci*, Pierre," and Chef Pierre bowed slightly before leaving the office. Napoleon jumped to his feet and returned the gesture with his own exaggerated bow. Chef Pierre glared down at Cora on his way out. She glared right back, unwilling to let him intimidate her.

"So you see, it was just a misunderstanding!" Monsieur Bocuse seemed awfully eager to explain away the situation. Cora wondered if she was the only one who noticed that Monsieur Bocuse seemed willing to forgive Chef for stealing, but without any proof, had thrown Jeanne out for the same crime. She wondered if even Monsieur Bocuse understood how unequally he was treating these two employees.

Monsieur Bocuse continued, "Now — *excusez moi* — I must return to helping serve lunch." He pointed them towards the door and walked them through the kitchen and out the back exit. He closed the door rather loudly behind them.

"How exciting!" Napoleon took off his hat, bowed low, and wandered over to grab his sandwich. "*Au revoir!*" he shouted at them before returning to the crowded street for more photo opportunities.

They'd reached a dead end.

9

CHAPTER NEUF

IN THE MARKET FOR INFORMATION

"Now what?" Jackson asked. He looked just as lost as Cora felt.

Jeanne raised her shoulders showing she had no idea. Bradley copied her. Cora took a deep breath, surveyed the parking lot, and got an idea.

"Okay, first," Cora started ticking things off on her fingers. "We need to find surveillance footage of that car Napoleon saw and cross-reference its license plate numbers to identify the driver, so we can demonstrate that it was NOT Chef Pierre's sister, proving he's a liar and our thief!" Cora finished, finger raised like Napoleon's saber, ready to charge into battle.

Mr. Doemner put his hand on Cora's shoulder. "Sweetie, I appreciate your enthusiasm, but there are a couple things. First, detectives aren't trying to prove someone is guilty; they are simply trying to figure out what really happened. Second, Chef Pierre has been with Monsieur Bocuse for many years. Auguste trusts him, and he admitted to giving his sister left-overs, but that doesn't make him our culprit, no matter how hateful he was to Jeanne."

"But we don't know for sure that's what happened. Are we just going to take Chef Pierre's word for it and ignore the fact that YOUR friend forgave Chef Pierre but not Jeanne when she is accused of the same thing!?" Cora demanded, stomping her foot.

"Honey, you know giving away leftovers and stealing inventory are not the same thing," her dad continued calmly. "While it doesn't feel fair, the best way we can help Jeanne here is to stay focused and not get wrapped up in our personal feelings. So let's get back to it."

Cora glared down at her notebook.

"There is a THIRD thing," Mr. Doemner continued. "I have not seen any surveillance cameras." He held up his hands, pointing at the tops of the roofs and gutters. "Nor did I see any inside. Monsieur Bocuse does not seem to have a security system in place."

"Maybe the city of Paris has some views of the street?" Cora asked.

"Even if they do, I don't think the Parisian police department will allow a 12-year old American girl to spy on their citizens for the sake of a few lost truffles."

Cora growled. "But, Dad! We can't let Pi— *the thief* — get away with this! Jeanne needs her job back!"

Mr. Doemner's phone suddenly chimed in his pocket. He pulled it out. "Text from Mom," he muttered, reading the words silently. He smiled, looking up. "She says she wrapped everything up and wants to jaunt over to Versailles to see the palace and grab dinner. Sound good?"

"No! Not good at all, Dad!" Cora retorted. "We only have two more days to solve this crime. We don't have time to 'enjoy dinner at a palace'," she fumed.

"My love," Mr. Doemner cajoled. "We reached a dead-end. No big deal. Maybe some time away from the situation will help you see things more clearly."

Cora looked at Jackson and Bradley, imploring them to support her. They agreed with their dad, mostly because they were hungry. She couldn't believe they would give up so easily.

"I want to stay and keep working on the case," she said.

"Cora, I can't just leave you to wander the streets of Paris by yourself."

"Why not? I'm twelve years old! It's daylight. It's not like I'm going to wander down any quiet dark alleys by myself."

"I could join her, Monsieur Doemner," Jeanne quietly volunteered, "I know the streets of Paris very well. I could have her back to your hotel before dark."

Cora's face lit up. "Really, Jeanne? Oh, Dad, please, please let me spend the rest of the day with Jeanne?"

Mr. Doemner looked at the two boys, evaluated the situation, and nodded. "Okay, Cora, you and Jeanne can keep working on the case here in the City. The boys and I will grab Mom to do some exploring and we'll meet back at the hotel for dinner around 6:00. Will that work?"

Cora jumped in the air, clapping her hands. "Yes! That sounds great!" Exploring Paris on her own with a real French woman seemed like a dream come true.

"Jeanne, please be sure you have your cell phone on and charged, and do not get separated from Cora. Cora, you have the address of the hotel written in your sketchbook, yes? You two can continue investigating, but you are not to go anywhere dangerous. Do you understand?" Mr. Doemner asked.

Jeanne and Cora confirmed.

Mr. Doemner took a deep breath. "Alright! Well, be safe, and we'll see you soon." He and the boys headed back to the street to wait for Mom to arrive in her taxi.

Jeanne looked down at Cora. "So? Where to?"

Cora pulled out her sketchbook. She had written down the address from the receipt for the truffles. "Do you know where this is?"

Jeanne typed the address into her phone. "*Oui! Marché Beauvau* is just past la Bastille."

"What's 'La Bastille'?" Cora asked as Jeanne requested an Uber to come pick them up.

"La Bastille was a French prison. During the French Revolution, the French people stormed the prison to gather the weapons and gunpowder they needed to overthrow the King. We now celebrate Bastille Day on July 14th, much the same way Americans celebrate their Independence Day on July 4th."

"You guys declared your independence ten days after we did?" Cora asked as they climbed into the back of a small car and headed towards the market.

Jeanne laughed. "Well, ten days and fourteen years later... Did you know it was the French who helped you win your war against the British?"

Cora nodded vaguely as she watched people on bicycles pass them, navigating the traffic. She thought it might be faster to walk as the Uber moved at a crawl.

The driver's radio played modern rock music, but Cora couldn't understand the French words. She drummed her fingers on the car seat, anxious to get to their destination.

The *Marché Beauvau* was hidden down a side street, its gray cobblestones lined with motorcycles. Cora was not very impressed until she walked past the iron gates and found herself surrounded by people and colors and smells.

Everywhere she looked, food was on display. Whole fish, pink and silver, lay on beds of ice next to baskets of oysters. Ropes of sausages hung under a sign that read *"Charcuterie"* with jars of golden honey and green olives sitting on the counter. Wooden trays advertised gleaming fruit and mounded vegetables in every color of the rainbow. Another shop (*'Boucher'*) featured thick red steaks and several enormous hams hanging from the ceiling. There was a whole store just dedicated to *'Fromage'* — cheese. Cora knew that was the shop where her parents would have spent most of their time (and money).

A guitarist perched on the edge of a fountain and his melody underlined the loud bustle of weekday shoppers haggling for the best deals. Cora threw a Euro into his open guitar case as she walked by and he winked at her in thanks.

Jeanne navigated them through the crowds, past a *fleuriste* where Cora wanted to stop and smell every single blossom. The aromas of roses and lilies wove amongst the smells of the cheese and fresh-baked bread. Cora relished the sights, sounds, and smells. THIS was exactly what she had hoped to find in France.

With Cora's mind still whirling, Jeanne stopped in front of a pristine shop that said *'Gastronomie'* on its navy blue awning. Cora looked down at the photo of the receipt on her phone: the name and address matched. She nodded up at Jeanne.

"Excusez moi," Jeanne said to the gentleman behind the counter, his back turned towards them as he restocked tall jars of oil and small tubs of butter. He turned, and Cora was instantly reminded

of her father: this man was also tall and broad with rosy cheeks and a thick brown beard. The man's dark brown eyes crinkled in the corners as he smiled at them, and Cora found herself smiling back.

"Ah, bonjour, mesdemoiselles! Puis-je vous aider?" he beamed.

Cora turned wide-eyed to Jeanne. She did not speak French and suddenly realized that she would require Jeanne's knowledge of the language to interview her suspects.

Jeanne seemed to understand Cora's concern, because she asked, *"Parlez vous anglais?"* placing her hand on Cora's back.

"Ah, *oui*!" he smiled down at Cora. "I speak English. *Un peu* - a little. How may I help you, young ladies?"

Cora sighed in relief. She said "Hi!" then changed it to *"Bonjour, monsieur*!" She figured it would be polite to at least try to speak his language as much as she knew how.

He seemed pleased by her attempt, and that made Cora feel better about asking her questions. She held up her sketchbook to the page with the information from the receipt, "Yesterday morning, you delivered some truffles to my friend's restaurant: Chez Bocuse."

The man took her book, pulling a pair of reading glasses from his apron pocket and placing them onto his nose so he could squint at her small writing. "Ah!" he made out the details at last. "Auguste! *Oui*, he is my friend as well," he said in his thick French accent. "Is something wrong with the truffles?" he asked as he handed Cora's book back to her.

Cora shifted her feet and cocked her head to one side. "Well, no. It sounds like the truffles were delicious. But yesterday afternoon, someone stole them from his restaurant."

The man's thick eyebrows knit together in concern. *"Non! C'est pas possible! Vraiment?"* He turned to Jeanne looking for confirmation.

Jeanne looked sad as she nodded. The man seemed genuinely upset by the news. He shook his head, pulling his glasses from his nose and returning them to his apron pocket. "*Désolé*, I am afraid I cannot replace them, even for a good friend like Auguste. We are sold out for the season."

Cora realized that he thought she was asking him for more truffles. "Oh no, we're not here to get more truffles," she explained. "We're trying to find out who took them."

This time the man's eyebrows shot up and he stepped back. "And you think that I…?" he asked, hand on his chest.

"Oh no!" Cora shook her head vigorously. *Geez, she was really bad at this whole interrogation thing.* "We just wondered where someone might go to sell two pounds — " she stopped and shifted to the metric system: " — a kilogram of truffles they had recently stolen?"

The man seemed confused, and Jeanne translated Cora's question into French. Probably adding some clarifying points, Cora thought, because it sounded longer coming from Jeanne and the man's eyes lost their storm clouds. He eventually nodded in understanding. Cora thought that she might let Jeanne do all of the questioning from now on.

"Ah, I see," he said. Then he seemed to consider the question, stroking his luxurious beard while squinting at the ceiling. Cora realized she was holding her breath when he finally frowned and said, "Well, I do not know them exactly," his look implying that he would not have anything to do with this particular person, "but I have heard that if you want something rare, and quickly, there are two brothers with a shop called 'Nowak' on la Rue Daguerre."

Jeanne swallowed hard enough for Cora to notice. She turned and saw Jeanne pulling up the map on her phone. "*À côté des Catacombes?*" she gasped.

"*Oui*," the man responded.

Cora caught the word "catacombs." The Catacombs had been one of the first places her dad had dragged them to when they arrived in Paris. She had shared Jeanne's shudder when he had told her that over six million people's bones had been buried in Paris' old limestone quarries, but she had been pleasantly surprised to discover the tour had been mostly... Boring. A very long walk through well-lit tunnels. Sure the tunnels were lined with skulls, but as Mom had pointed out: "No matter how different we think we are in life, we are all the same in death."

After staring at two miles of old bones, Cora agreed. *It does not matter if we are rich or poor, Christian or Muslim, black or white... After a couple centuries, we all look the same,* Cora thought.

She patted Jeanne's arm. "It's okay, Jeanne. We don't have to go into the catacombs... Do we?" she looked at the shop owner to confirm.

He grinned, "*Non*. Their shop is a block away."

Jeanne took a deep breath and looked down at Cora. "Okay, let's go."

Cora turned to the man. "*Merci beaucoup*," she said carefully. He smiled broadly, "*De rien!*"

The girls walked back out into the street, but Cora thought that it seemed just a little darker. Grabbing Jeanne's hand, she told herself to be brave.

10

CHAPTER DIX

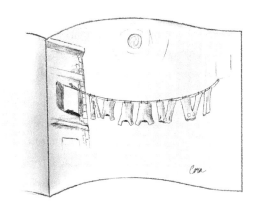

HAND CAUGHT IN THE TRUFFLE JAR

Fifteen minutes later, they were standing on a cobblestone street so narrow the cab had to back out the way he came in after he dropped them off.

Cora noticed immediately that this neighborhood felt completely different from the manicured, bustling hotel where her family stayed, just streets away. The faces that passed her on the street here were harder, their clothes worn. There was trash in the gutters, but everyone here seemed to belong and have a purpose, like they were going to work or visiting a friend.

Children ran along the road, weaving in and around the vendor's carts. A *grandmaman* yelled at them from a tiny balcony, laundry on a line moving in the breeze. Cora didn't understand her words, but she guessed it was something like, "HEY KIDS! Cut it out!" The wrinkled face of the woman was framed by grey hair that escaped from her bun in the breeze as she scowled and wagged her finger. Maybe grandmothers were the same in every country.

The girls stood in front of their destination. Cora wished they were standing in front of any other shop. The Nowak store seemed to be a black hole where the "messy but friendly" vibe she got from the rest of the street disappeared. Cora felt a chill run through her, even though the sun had not yet set.

The other shops were open with bored vendors sitting behind tables, offering wares like sunglasses, necklaces, or hot food, to the occasional tourist who got lost and wandered down their lane. Comparatively, the Nowak store looked like a fortress. Two windows guarded either side of the door, covered in posters advertising cheap cell phone rates and foot cream. The windows and door were all covered in black metal bars and Cora wondered if the owner was trying to keep people out or in.

Cora's palms felt sweaty as she looked at Jeanne. "Well?" she asked.

"We're here," Jeanne murmured. Her smile looked nervous, like she was trying to be brave for Cora's sake. That made Cora more determined than ever to hide her fear. She took a deep breath and pulled open the door, hearing a small chime announce her entrance as she stepped into the darkened interior. She jumped when the hanging blinds crashed into place after Jeanne closed the door.

It looked like a poorly-lit mini-mart, with two rows of shelves stretching towards the back. One of the long fluorescent bulbs overhead blinked so rapidly that Cora had to squint her eyes. A low counter stood to their right as they entered, with a teenage boy sitting behind the cash register, his feet propped up on a pile of papers. The boy's blond hair covered his right eye. He looked up at them with a bored glance, murmured "*Bonjour*" and returned to staring at his cell phone.

Cora decided to look around before asking any questions. Maybe she could find a clue.

The old metal shelves were crammed with all kinds of random items. As Cora wandered down the center aisle, she couldn't help running her fingers over the French foods — smooth jars of *confit*, crinkly cellophane bags of chocolates tied with ribbon, cold tins of *foie gras*, cardboard boxes of crackers, and bottles of wine. All of them seemed past their expiration date, with bright stickers announcing big discounts.

The sandy linoleum flooring had started to peel up at the corners and the flickering bulbs threw strange shadows around everything she touched. Cora felt the hairs rise on the backs of her arms. Something was here. She could feel it.

As she and Jeanne reached the back of the store, Cora noticed a plain white door off to the left with a black and gold placard that read "*Employés Seulement.*" Jeanne confirmed that it meant "Employees Only." Cora started to walk past, looking for her jar of truffles, when she noticed a peep hole in the center of the door.

That was strange. Why would someone need to see OUT of the back room? Who was spying on the mini-mart from inside the mini-mart?

Cora looked back towards the counter at the front. The shelves blocked her view of the boy, but she found herself staring straight into the Cyclopean black eye of a security camera. Why was the security camera watching the back door, not the front?

Cora glanced down at her ring. Grey as a stormcloud. Something big was brewing. She pulled Jeanne down where neither the camera nor the peep-hole could see them, far enough away so the boy in the front couldn't hear.

"I need you to distract him," Cora whispered, nodding her head in the boy's direction.

Jeanne's eyebrows furrowed. "*Pourquoi?*"

Cora looked meaningfully at the door.

"Oh no," Jeanne shook her head. "You cannot go back there by yourself. Your Papa and Maman would kill me!"

"Well, *I* can't distract him!" Cora explained. "I don't speak French!"

Jeanne opened her mouth to continue her objections, but Cora waved her hand in dismissal. "I'll be just fine," she insisted. "Just go chat with the boy and I'll be back out here in less than five minutes."

"Five minutes?" Jeanne squeaked. "I cannot talk to a boy for five minutes." Cora noticed Jeanne seemed genuinely terrified by the prospect.

"Yes, you can. You'll be fine. Ask him about…" Cora scrunched up her lips, thinking. "Well, I guess you might as well ask him about truffles!" Maybe the shop clerk would lead them right to their prize.

Jeanne's eyes got wide.

"It's okay! He's not the thief," Cora reassured her. "He probably bought the truffles without even realizing they were stolen. He's got no reason to hide."

"Fine, but what if he needs to get them from the back of the store?" Jeanne pointed at the door.

Cora had not considered that. "Well, then, talk loudly as you get close and I'll find someplace to hide once I'm in there."

She had no idea what she would be walking into, but she was small and flexible. Cora felt confident she could hide behind whatever she found on the other side.

Jeanne jumped up and down like she was getting ready to run a race, muttered "*Mon dieu*" under her breath, and walked awkwardly to the front of the store. Cora peeked her head around the edge of the aisle. Jeanne cleared her throat. "*Excusez-moi…*"

As soon as the boy's eyes were firmly on Jeanne, Cora slipped noiselessly through the back door.

She paused as the ray of light from the shop compressed into a single beam and then winked out as the door clicked shut behind her. She gulped.

The back of the store looked nothing like the front. Everything was cold, dark and immaculately clean. The ceiling rose at least three stories up and Cora could see a pleated steel delivery door directly opposite her.

Thick cardboard boxes lined the industrial-strength shelves that filled the space. Cora tried to pull open one of the boxes nearest her but they were all taped shut. She couldn't read the labels, except one that said "*poison*" which she was pretty sure meant the same thing in English.

Cora told herself she could slip between two boxes if she needed to hide, but how in the world was she going to find a jar of truffles in all of this?

She tiptoed down the aisle. Goosebumps thrilled down her spine. The boxes stared down at her, watching every step.

At the end of the shelves stood a massive shredder, which she knew people used to destroy confidential information. It looked like a meat-grinder and Cora wondered: *What could they possibly need to destroy that requires a machine big enough to swallow small children?*

She looked around and glanced inside the bin. Lying on top of the confetti paper was a crumpled yellow receipt, like someone had intended to shred it, but hadn't bothered to turn on the machine.

Cora smoothed open the paper. A generic *"Reçu"* was printed on the top and Cora could make out a scribbled "Wenecja" and "TACDIII." She started to toss it back into the trash can, but instinct placed it into her pocket at the last moment.

She looked around and spotted a large silver refrigerator off in the corner, to the right of the loading-dock door. She crept closer. The large silver doors were scuffed and dented. It looked ancient and rattled as it hummed, like it was having trouble breathing.

She wrapped her fingers around the handle and prepared to pull it open when a small patch of dark fur ran out from underneath the fridge, scurried between her feet and dashed under a wash bucket and mop. Cora could not help it: she screamed. More of a yelp, really, but it echoed in the huge empty warehouse. She cringed, then decided she had to hurry.

She yanked open the door. There, at her eye level, was a large glass jar of rice filled with what looked like seriously deformed yellow potatoes.

"Hey!" a man's voice shouted behind Cora.

She whirled around, slamming the door closed.

11

CHAPTER ONZE

12-YEAR OLD GOURMET

Across from her sat an office. She had missed it completely because the wall closest to her had been covered in boxes. The office's door, which faced the delivery gate in the back, stood open and an older man with thin white hair combed over his freckled scalp stomped towards her.

"*Qu'est-ce que tu fais?*" the man demanded as he came closer.

Cora froze. She didn't understand French, but she could guess what he meant. She swallowed. Should she run for the street? Or stay and try to explain herself?

She had just found the truffles! She could not just walk away. As she had explained to Jeanne, this man probably had not stolen the truffles; he was probably just the "fence" who had bought the truffles and planned to resell them.

She took a deep breath and decided to use the little French Jeanne had taught her. *"Bonjour Monsieur,"* she said.

Be polite, her dad always insisted. *People will respect you when they sense you respect them.*

"Parlez vous anglais?" She remembered Jeanne asking the other shop-keeper if he spoke English.

The man pulled up short. He shook his head. *"Non. Qui êtes-vous?"*

Cora had exhausted her French words. Her mouth hung open with no sounds coming out, when the front door of the shop flew open and the boy from the cash register barged in, looking annoyed, followed quickly by Jeanne, who looked sheepish.

A flurry of French passed back and forth between the old man and the younger, who finally rolled his eyes, threw up his hands and returned to the shop. Jeanne walked quickly to Cora's side.

"Bonjour," she offered the old man, who now looked less angry and more curious about his two unexpected guests.

Cora really wished her parents were there. They were good at navigating sticky situations. *How would Mom and Dad handle this?* Cora wondered to herself.

Smile.

In all their travels, Cora's mom and dad had pointed out that smiling is universal. Not too much, not too little. *Be friendly, not crazy,* Mom's voice echoed in her head.

Cora took a deep breath, smiled in her most reassuring "I'm-Total-ly-Trustworthy" way and held out her hand. *"Je m'appelle Cora,"* she announced. Jeanne cringed a little at her accent, but it seemed to work.

The man's lips twitch in response. He shook Cora's outstretched hand, and answered, *"Je m'appelle Antony Nowak."*

"Pourquoi cherches-tu dans mon réfrigérateur?" he asked, pointing at the cooler. Cora picked up on the word "refrigerator" and had to think quickly. Should she be honest? Play dumb? To buy herself some time, she looked at Jeanne expectantly. Jeanne translated: "Why are you looking in my refrigerator?"

Cora nodded, as if understanding for the first time. She felt incredibly grateful for Jeanne's presence — having an interpreter would buy her time, even if she had been fluent in French!

"I'm looking for truffles," Cora said.

Jeanne translated. The man raised his eyebrows: *"Aimes-tu truffes?"*

"You like truffles?" Jeanne explained.

"Oui," Cora answered, proud that she remembered the word for 'Yes.' "You have some very nice ones. Where did you get them?"

She waited while Jeanne turned her words into French and she picked out the words "Alba, Italie" from the man's response. He moved past her to open the refrigerator, pulled out the jar, fished out one of the potato-looking objects and held it out to Cora.

"He says they come from Alba, Italy. They are the finest specimens he's received in years. He wants you to smell one," Jeanne shrugged.

Cora hesitantly took the small cream-colored fungi with dirty knobs growing all over it. THIS was the thing that caused all this trouble? She held it up to her nose and took a sniff. EW! It smelled like someone had shoved garlic into a gym sock and buried it in the dirt. Her eyes started to water and she pulled it away from her nose with a cough.

The man chuckled.

Cora remembered that she was supposed to like truffles and forced a smile onto her face. "Mmmm…" she grimaced.

She did not know how to explain that she didn't mean "Where did the truffles come from?" she meant "Who sold you the truffles?" At least not without arousing suspicion.

Then she spotted a video camera in the top corner of the warehouse.

Maybe she did not need to ask him… She looked at Jeanne and wondered how she could get them out of the situation as quickly as possible.

Cora turned to the man. "How much?" she asked, holding up the truffle.

"*C'est combien?*" Jeanne translated.

But the man was already nodding. Evidently, he understood the question. Suddenly Cora wondered if he had figured out the same secret she had discovered — that feigning ignorance bought you precious minutes during negotiations.

"*Trois cents,*" he said. "300," Jeanne explained.

"Three HUNDRED dollars??" Cora exclaimed.

"Euros," Jeanne corrected.

"Whatever," Cora waved away the distinction. "300 Euros for this stinky knob of fungus??"

Now, the man looked like he understood — and was annoyed.

Cora remembered that she was playing the part of a sophisticated gourmand who loved truffles, and cleared her throat. "I mean… Is that all?"

She very carefully placed the ridiculously-expensive truffle back into the jar of rice. "Very nice," she said to Mr. Nowak, with another pained smile.

Jeanne shifted her feet as the man screwed the lid back on and returned it to the refrigerator. He turned around, arms crossed over his chest, as if waiting for an explanation.

Cora sucked in her cheeks and looked around the shop. "Well, uh… *Merci.* Thank you. This has been great! We'll be back with, uh, 300 Euros." With that, she turned away from the man and started walking towards the shop exit.

Jeanne bowed slightly, reiterated, "*Merci,*" and Cora half expected him to follow them as they hurried to the door. But he didn't. He just scratched his head, grinned, and returned to his office.

Cora released an explosive breath of relief when they finally closed the door behind them. Safely back in the Mini-Mart.

Now, for the second part of her plan.

"Let's go," Cora said. "*Allons-y?*"

"*Oui.*" Jeanne grinned, "*allons-y.*"

She led them through the aisles and they walked out the front door, setting off the same bell. Just as they got to the sidewalk, Cora stopped, patted her pockets, and said, "Hmm… I think I might have set my phone down. Let me go back and check!"

Jeanne looked like she was going to join her, but Cora waved her away. "No, I'm fine! I'll just be a sec," and she ducked back into the shop.

She had not forgotten her phone.

12

CHAPTER DOUZE

WHAT A PAIR OF BLUE EYES CAN DO

Cora had noticed the small video screen, showing the security cameras, sitting on the counter by the boy. He did not look up when she came back in, so she cleared her throat: "Ahem!"

He looked up, one eyebrow raised.

"*Excusez-moi.*" She smiled her most charming smile. "*Parlez vous anglais?*" she tried again.

He nodded with a confused expression.

She pointed at the video screen. "Can you show me who brought those truffles yesterday?"

He blinked.

She decided to try again. "Can… you….show…" she used her hands to point at him and then wave at the video screen, hoping she could get him to understand her meaning using charades.

"I heard you," he said in perfect English. "Why would I do that?"

Cora swallowed. *Here goes nothing*, she thought. "Well, because I am a private detective and I'm trying to establish an alibi for my client." She gestured in the general direction of Jeanne.

The boy just stared at her, both eyebrows raised. Cora nodded, as if that would reinforce her story. "So, if you could just rewind the tape, and let me see who delivered the truffles… that would really help… me…. out." Her bravado dwindled by the moment.

He just stared at her.

She swallowed and then remembered a movie scene and reached into her pocket. Her dad had given her 50 Euros "for emergencies." This was definitely an emergency.

She slid the orange note across the counter. "It would mean a lot to me," she said with her sweetest smile.

Eyeing the money, then looking back to Cora, he grabbed the bill, and turned towards the little screen. He moved a mouse and a menu appeared on the screen. "It's not a tape," he muttered as he clicked on a couple things. Cora waited, but he didn't explain himself. He pulled up a folder with yesterday's date and Cora saw about fifteen files listed.

He said, "Do you know when your friend…?"

Cora thought back to the timecard and how far they were from the restaurant. "Sometime after 4pm?" she suggested.

He pushed the hair out of his eyes and double clicked on a video. "This one starts at 4:50."

Cora must have looked confused, because the boy added, "The recording is motion-activated."

She nodded, not entirely sure she understood, but grateful the boy had agreed to look. The black and white film showed a couple who walked in, looked around briefly and left.

Cora shook her head. "Not it."

The boy clicked on the last file, "5:20."

Several teenagers came in to buy cigarettes and chat with the boy behind the counter. He blushed and hurriedly shut the video: "Not it."

Cora paused, looking through the times. There was one at 3:15. She pointed: "That one?"

Sure enough, the grainy footage revealed a short, chubby man who walked into the store, carrying a bag. Cora held her breath. Could she be that lucky? Was that Pierre? Had he managed to get here on his break, so quickly?

But as he turned towards the camera, she realized it definitely was not Pierre. His t-shirt said: "What's not to Louvre about Paris?" and his bag was probably for the enormous camera that hung around his neck. Tourist.

No luck.

She paused. The boy seemed willing to let her try again, even though she'd struck out three times.

"What about today?" she ventured. "Who was the first person in?"

The boy muttered something about "strange alibi" but obligingly pulled up today's footage. The first video was marked at 5:15am.

The man she had met in the back room came out, unlocked the front door and escorted a petite woman with a dark polka-dotted headscarf and large sunglasses towards the back of the store. She carried what could very easily be a large glass jar. They disappeared through the back door into the warehouse. The next recording started at 5:27 when the lady re-emerged without anything in her arms.

Cora silently willed the woman to look up towards the camera, but she pulled her scarf too far forward, and the sunglasses covered most of her face. She intentionally turned away from the camera, as if she knew it was there and didn't want to be recorded.

That must be the thief, but Cora didn't know what to make of what she saw. "Is there a corresponding video in the back?"

The boy shook his head. "You'd have to ask my Dad for that," he nodded towards the back of the store.

She was about to ask to watch the tape again, but jumped when the door opened and the chime went off. Jeanne came in. "Did you find your phone?" she asked.

Cora looked at Jeanne's headscarf and swallowed, nodding quickly. She held up her phone, which had been in her back pocket the whole time. "Yep!" she said with forced brightness. "*Allons-y!*" she added with gusto, holding her hand towards the door, urging Jeanne to return outdoors. Jeanne laughed and went through the door.

Cora turned quickly. "*Merci beaucoup!*" she said to the boy. "That helped a lot."

The boy's lips twitched slightly. "*De rien,*" he said. His bright blue eyes lit up over the weak smile. Cora could not help but think that those blue eyes looked very familiar as she followed Jeanne outside.

13

CHAPTER TREIZE

A HOUSE DIVIDED

That night, back in their hotel suite, Cora listened as her parents showed her all their pictures of Versailles.

"...and this is the Hall of Mirrors."

Mr. Doemner had connected his camera to the hotel's television. A photo of a long ballroom, covered in gold with large crystal chandeliers glittered on the screen. Cora's mind was distracted, but she had to admit, it looked pretty glorious.

"They brought in mirror-makers from Venice, the only place that knew how to make mirrors. This room alone has 357 mirrors," her mom explained.

"Then they were all assassinated!" Bradley yelled, a huge grin on his face.

Cora looked at her dad, eyebrows raised. Bradley often made up crazy facts. Mr. Doemner nodded in confirmation. "The artists, not the mirrors, were all killed. Evidently the Venetians weren't happy that someone sold out their secrets."

"Intense," Cora replied tonelessly, dropping her head to rest on her crossed arms at the kitchen table.

Mr. Doemner continued the presentation, but her mom came over and placed her hand on Cora's head. "Are you feeling okay, honey? How did everything go today?"

Cora shrugged. She didn't know what she'd found and she wasn't sure where to go next.

Her mom pulled up a chair at the table next to her. "What did you and Jeanne do?"

Mr. Doemner continued to scroll through the photos, but stopped narrating, as if listening for Cora's response. The boys continued playing cards on the sofa, oblivious.

She walked them through the day and by the time she got to the videotape, her entire family had gathered at the table to hear her story.

"A WOMAN stole the truffles?" Bradley asked.

"And she was wearing a headscarf?" Mrs. Doemner pressed.

Cora did not want to, but she nodded *Yes.*

"You're sure it wasn't…?" Mrs. Doemner paused.

Cora shook her head. Her heart broke thinking of the possibility that hung heavily in the room. With a tear perched in the corner of her eye, she admitted, "I don't know."

" Oh gosh, I hate to even ask this out loud… *Could* it have been Jeanne?" Mr. Doemner asked.

"What?" Bradley exclaimed, just figuring out what they were talking about. "No way! We love Jeanne. Jeanne could NOT have stolen the truffles."

The salty drop dislodged itself from Cora's eye and rolled down her cheek. That fear had kept her quiet on the whole drive back to her apartment. Jeanne had asked her if everything was okay, and Cora had nodded, but…

"What if I was wrong?" she cried, finally voicing her fears aloud, "What if it was Jeanne and I asked you to spend a lot of money to save a *thief*?" The dam broke and the waterworks fell.

"Oh sweetie," Mrs. Doemner pulled Cora into a hug. "It's not your fault. Shh…" she ran her hands over Cora's back as she sobbed against her chest.

"Quit it, guys. It's not Jeanne," Bradley said, crossing his arms and pursing his lips.

"What did she look like?" Mr. Doemner asked.

Cora sat up, mentally reviewing the tape. "It's hard to tell how tall she was because the camera angle was from up above. But she could maybe see over the shelves if she stood on her tiptoes. Fairly skinny. Dark clothes. The head scarf had white polka dots."

"But you couldn't see her face?"

Cora shook her head. "It was like she knew the camera was there and used her scarf to cover her face and hair."

Mrs. Doemner chewed on her lip. "Well, the description feels like it could be her height and weight, but we've never seen Jeanne in a patterned scarf."

Her dad asked: "Did the shop boy seem like he recognized Jeanne?"

Cora's eyes brightened. "No! He didn't seem to recognize her at all!"

"Maybe that's part of the act," Jackson suggested.

Bradley scowled at him.

"Or he's new," Jackson added.

This time Bradley got up and came over to smack Jackson on the arm. "It's NOT Jeanne!" he shouted.

"Hey hey," Mr. Doemner interjected. "No hitting, buddy." He pulled Bradley onto his lap. "Of course we don't want Jeanne to be the thief, but as I reminded Cora yesterday, our job is to find the truth, wherever that leads. Then afterwards, we can decide what to— "

"That's it!" Cora shouted, laughing. She stood up. "It must have been Chef Pierres' SISTER!" she crowed.

"That's exactly NOT what I said," Mr. Doemner responded.

Cora started pacing, the engines in her head going full throttle. "Chef Pierre must have given her the truffles in the bag and had her sell them the next morning."

"Didn't Chef Pierre say it was just leftovers he gave his sister?" her mom asked.

"Of course that's what he would *say*," Cora sneered. "But he can't prove it!"

"Neither can we," Jackson pointed out.

That paused Cora, and she sat down on the arm of the sofa to think.

"What did you say the shop owner's name was?" Mr. Doemner asked.

"Anthony Nowak," Cora muttered.

"Why does that name seem familiar…?" her dad asked, stroking his beard.

Jackson's eyes opened wide. He stood up and ran to their bedroom. He returned, carrying Cora's "Case Journal," a very official-looking teal notebook with purple sequin stars glued to the cover. Cora copied her notes from her sketchbook into this journal every night, adding any details she remembered. He flipped through the pages, then stopped, dropping the diary onto the table with a dramatic flair. He pointed at the timecard where Cora had copied:

"Leo Nowak."

Cora gasped. Dad's eyebrows flew up. Mom seemed confused: "Who's Leo?"

"Cora's crush," Mr. Doemner explained.

"Ohhh?" Mrs. Doemner crooned with a mischievous grin at Cora. Then realization dawned. "Ohhh…" she said with a frown. "Oh, that's not good."

Bradley finally caught up. "Wait. So *Leo* stole the truffles?"

"No!" Cora declared. "No way. I'm sure there are PLENTY of people whose last name is Nowak." But the thought of the shop boy's blue eyes haunted her.

"Besides," she added, reassuring herself as much as anyone. "It was a woman in the video."

"Maybe Leo dressed up as a woman!" Bradley suggested.

Cora glared at him. "If it was Leo and he was selling the stolen truffles to his — What? Father? Uncle? Brother? — Why would he dress up?" she demanded.

"Or he and Jeanne are working together," Jackson said with darkness in his voice.

Every eye whipped to Jackson. "What do you mean?" Mr. Doemner asked.

"Well," Jackson said, sitting forward in his chair. "We know Leo was the last one to see the truffles." Cora now glared at Jackson. "Maybe he hid them in his car last night, and expressed sympathy in the refrigerator to distract attention from his accomplice, who he would take to sell the goods for him the next day, because he didn't want his family to know he was involved."

"But if Jeanne was involved," Bradley said, "Why wouldn't she have given them to the police when they threatened to arrest her?"

"Exactly," Cora said. "None of that makes any sense. You know what *does* make sense? Chef Pierre was lying and it was his sister who I saw in the video," Cora insisted.

"But how could we prove that?" her dad asked.

Bradley said, "We should dust the jar for fingerprints!"

Cora seemed ready to hop on board with that suggestion when Jackson pointed out, "Uh... Everyone touched that jar. We would find everyone's fingerprints. Except maybe Jeanne's, if she wasn't the thief," he paused, thinking it through. "Unless the thief wore gloves, in which case the absence of fingerprints would be the evidence of guilt." He shook his head, "No that doesn't work..."

"And even if you did get good fingerprints off the jar," Mrs. Doemner mentioned, "we'd have to collect everyone else's fingerprints to compare them to. And I don't know anyone who would voluntarily give their fingerprints to a private investigator."

Cora was grateful her mom didn't call them "kids." Despite only being twelve years old, she felt like a real detective.

"We could steal their fingerprints using glasses, like they do in the spy movies!" Bradley suggested.

"Yeah!" Cora liked that idea. "We could sneak into the kitchen and steal their water cups. Or Mom and Dad could buy some really expensive champagne and give each staff member a glass and then we could collect them afterwards..."

"That's a great idea," Mr. Doemner interrupted as he saw Cora spending more money, "but even if we got all the kitchen staff's prints, what are we trying to prove?"

Cora sighed. "You're right. We need to figure out a different way to catch Pierre's sister!"

Mr. Doemner shook his head. "Okay, let's go back: What do we know for sure?"

Cora grabbed her Case Journal from Jackson and made a list:

1. Truffles disappeared before dinner on Tuesday
2. Woman sold truffles to Anthony Nowak at 5:15am on Wednesday

Jackson looked over Cora's shoulder as she wrote. He pointed at the second line and said, "'Person wearing a headscarf' would be more accurate than 'Woman'."

Cora aggressively underlined her word choice several times. "Of course it was a woman! Leo is Daddy's height with really large muscles," she held her hands out from her shoulders as if putting on football pads. Mrs. Doemner smirked at the detailed description.

Jackson rolled his eyes.

"Seriously, the only reason we're suspecting Leo is because he has the same last name as the shop — " Cora stopped suddenly, her face going white.

"What?" Mom asked.

Cora turned to her dad. "Leo mentioned that his uncle got him the job. Remember?"

Mr. Doemner slowly nodded. "That's right."

Cora rubbed her face, thinking. "But still!" she said at last, looking up. "Even if that explains how the thief knew to go there, it definitely wasn't Leo in the video."

"But she knew where the camera was located," Jackson pointed out. "So it seems likely that whoever she was, was Leo's accomplice. And Leo seemed intent on defending Jeanne during your conversation."

Bradley picked up the implication and stood up on his chair. "It was NOT Jeanne!" he shouted, as if more volume would convince his family of the truth.

"You're right, Bradley. It was Chef Pierre's sister," Cora stated.

"Oh my gosh, Cora," Jackson was becoming exasperated. "Just because it makes the people you like innocent, doesn't mean it's true!" He continued talking over her as she started to argue. "Besides, the whole point is to PROVE the thing, and we have no way to prove Chef Pierre did anything except give his hungry sister food that no one else wanted! You obviously don't like him…."

"Because he is a *Caca Boudin!*" Cora shouted, interrupting Jackson. Mrs. Doemner laughed, snorting wine through her nose, and had to set down her wine glass.

"A what?" Jackson demanded.

"Where did you learn *'caca boudin,'* Cora?" Mrs. Doemner asked, wiping her face with a napkin.

Cora turned red. "I heard some kids in the street near the Nowak store fighting. One of them called the other *'caca boudin.'* When Jeanne told me what it meant, I thought: That's the perfect way to describe someone as mean and bigoted as Chef Pierre."

"But what does it mean?" Jackson asked.

"Poop sausage. Apparently French has a swear word just for kids," Cora said with a twisted grin.

"Well, then, you are being a *caca boudin*, Cora! Not a good detective," Jackson taunted and slapped her shoulder. Cora lunged.

"Whoa, whoa, whoa!" Mr. Doemner stood up as Cora and Jackson started grappling with each other on the kitchen floor. He pushed them apart and said, "Cora, we do not use that kind of language.

While I agree that Chef Pierre seems quite racist and prejudiced, and that makes him not very likeable, it does not make him a thief."

Cora glared at her father.

He left one hand on her shoulder as he turned to Jackson. "And Jackson, we do not call people names, nor do we hit people. Please say you're sorry."

Jackson clamped his mouth shut.

"Okay, time out until you're ready to apologize," his dad said, taking Jackson's hand and drawing him towards the bedroom. Jackson started crying, which made Cora laugh. Jackson screamed, "Stop laughing at me!" which only made her laugh harder. She stuck out her tongue, and even though she immediately regretted it, Bradley came up and slugged Cora in the arm to defend Jackson's honor.

"Okay! That's it!" Mrs. Doemner shouted through the chaos. "No more detective-ing." Jackson and Cora stopped and looked at her: "What?" "Nooo!" Bradley burst into tears. Mrs. Doemner just shook her head. "Look at you guys being mean to each other. That's not okay! I liked you guys showing initiative and working as a team to solve a puzzle, but when it turns you against one another, it's time to stop."

Bradley started to wail even louder and now Cora joined him. "But Mom! We have to solve the crime! You always tell us to never give up! We can't FAIL!"

"I also tell you that failure is just a learning lesson. And what I want you to learn most importantly is that your family comes first. Being kind is more important than being right."

"But…"

"Nope! No but's. We're all done. We're going to go up the Eiffel Tower tomorrow and then we'll come home to pack, since we leave on Friday."

All three kids let out a howl of protest.

"No arguing," Mr. Doemner bellowed over the din. "Boys, I want you guys to take a quick bath before bed. Cora, if you want to soak in Mom and Dad's tub, you can." He kept talking loudly and shepherded them towards their respective rooms, despite the protests. Then he closed the doors to the bedrooms behind the kids to drown out their whining, and came back to the kitchen table.

He handed Mrs. Doemner her glass of red wine, and clinked it with his own, saying, "So much for French *fraternité*."

Mrs. Doemner grinned, and they both drained their glasses.

14

CHAPTER QUATORZE

ALL'S FAIR IN LOVE AND WAR

Cora was still fuming that she wasn't sleuthing, but as the elevators opened and she stepped out onto the observation deck at the top of the Eiffel Tower, she had to admit that it was pretty cool.

"When it opened in 1889," Mr. Doemner said, walking over to the nearest windows, "this was the tallest tower in the world."

Cora could believe it. Blue sky and billowing clouds draped over the white and green city, which stretched as far as she could see in every direction. The silver River Seine wound around them like a giant serpent, grey-banded with bridges. Roads radiated in all directions from where they stood, cars scurrying along them like colorful beetles.

Only a wire net protected them from the 900 foot drop. Tourists swarmed everywhere, snapping photos and Cora was almost grateful it was so crowded, because the people blocked some of the wind that whistled past the spire.

Bradley bounced around the perimeter, pointing at things they had seen. Across the river to the west, beyond le *Jardins du Trocadero* Bradley spotted "The Aquarium!" And just beyond the Aquarium, bit towards the north: "The Arc de Triomphe!"

"Where?" Cora asked, coming to stand behind her brother.

"There!" he pointed, and sure enough, as his finger followed the curve of a large avenue, she saw the stone monument. It looked like a tiny Lego-piece from here, but she had really enjoyed climbing it and taking pictures of the city.

Mrs. Doemner walked up behind her. "All our photos from the Eiffel Tower are going to look weird, because the Eiffel Tower isn't in the shot!" She laughed. "No one will believe this is Paris!" She grinned down at Cora. Cora scowled and walked to a different part of the platform. She was not yet ready to forgive her mother for ruining her chance of solving the mystery and clearing an innocent girl.

· · ·

An hour later, back on the ground, they began walking through the lawns of the *Champ de Mars* towards *École Militaire* because Mr. Doemner loved all things Military History.

"What do you think *Champ de Mars* means?" Mrs. Doemner quizzed Jackson.

"Champion of Mars?" he guessed.

"Close! Champ comes closer to 'Camp' or 'Campus' of Mars. These lawns were the marching grounds for the French military." She turned to Cora. "And who was Mars?"

Cora rolled her eyes. "The god of war. The Roman equivalent of the Greek Ares," she recited. She had been in love with mythology since she could learn how to read. *Who was Mars?* Too easy!

Mr. Doemner interjected, "That's how we got the word 'martial' for all things war-related, like 'martial law.'"

"And martians?" Bradley asked as he tried to climb a lamppost.

Dad laughed, but Cora was the one who said, "Martians came from the planet Mars, also named after the god of war."

Jackson asked, "Why'd they name it after a god of war?"

"Well, do you remember when we looked at Mars through our telescope?" his mom asked. Jackson nodded. "What color was it?"

"Red."

"Yep. The color of blood, shed during battle," Mrs. Doemner explained.

My family is so weird, Cora thought with a secretly proud smile. She had her sketchpad out and was studying the people around her, looking for a good subject to draw.

One young couple had squished themselves together, holding out their selfie-stick, evidently trying to get the angle of the Eiffel Tower "just right" above their heads. She didn't understand what they were saying; their language sounded harsh and guttural after the lilting melodic French language she had been hearing all week.

As her family kept walking, they passed a large group of older tourists who seemed to be on a group tour, taking turns posing in front of the Eiffel Tower until everyone got a photo of themselves pointing at, holding up, or otherwise emphasizing the Tower behind them.

Her eyes almost missed the couple sitting on the far edge of the lawn, but Cora always looked for pattern-interrupts, and the blond head leaning against the bright purple headscarf was definitely unique. She stopped dead in her tracks.

Bradley ran into her with an "Oof!" and a "Hey! Cora!"

Mr. and Mrs. Doemner turned back to see what had caused the kerfuffle. Cora just pointed. The whole family turned their attention towards the couple on the bench.

"Jeanne!" Bradley exclaimed, excited to see his friend again, and he ran over the grass and through a bush to get to her.

He had already hugged her and shared that he had tried to eat all of her cookies last night but Mom was worried he would get a tummy ache which was silly because he never got tummy aches from eating sugar, when the family joined him.

"*Bonjour*!" Mrs. Doemner said, extending her hand to Jeanne.

"Leo, good to see you," Mr. Doemner added, shaking hands with the man now standing next to Jeanne. Leo had jumped to his feet when the Doemners walked up, eyes wide and blushing red.

"Good to see you too, *Monsieur*," Leo replied, shaking his hand.

Cora just stared at the two of them. Obviously together. Obviously more than just work acquaintances.

"Why didn't you tell us you were a couple?" Cora blurted out. As her mom and dad turned to stare at her, she realized that she was being rude, but she did not care. If they had withheld this key detail, what else had they been hiding?

Leo scratched his head, "Well, uh…" but Jeanne interrupted: "It was me. My family does not approve of Leo, so I asked him to keep this a secret." She looked at Leo as if silently apologizing.

"But why keep it a secret from *us*?" Cora practically shouted. "We've been trying to clear your name, and here you two are," she waved her arms at the two of them, "the primary suspects just sitting here — "

"Wait. We are your primary suspects?" Leo interjected.

"Yes!" Cora exploded. She had fought so hard to prove Leo and Jeanne were innocent and they had betrayed her trust. "Leo was the last one to see the truffles and Jeanne was the last one in the shop, alone and unsupervised. And then I saw a video of a woman in a headscarf selling the truffles in *your* Nowak shop!"

It had only been a guess, but the way Leo blanched when she mentioned the shop, she knew from the sinking feeling in her stomach that it was true. He *was* related to the people in that shop.

"What?" Jeanne asked. "You saw a video? When?" Her forehead pressed together in lines. *Probably worried we discovered her secret,* Cora seethed.

Cora took a deep breath. "When I went back into the shop to look for my phone. I asked the boy at the counter — a boy who looks an awful lot like Leo," she added with her eyebrow raised at Leo, " — to show me the surveillance video footage."

Jeanne's mouth hung open. Cora went on. "At 5:15am on Wednesday, a woman wearing a headscarf entered the shop carrying a jar. She headed straight for the back room and exited a short time later without a jar."

"And you think it was... *me* in the video?" Jeanne asked.

Cora shrugged. "We couldn't tell who it was. She knew where the camera was and pulled the scarf over her face. Which would make sense if someone had told her where it would be." She looked pointedly at Leo again. The theory she had been fighting against so strongly was suddenly feeling like the most obvious solution.

"*N'importe quoi!*" Leo exclaimed. "Jeanne did not steal the truffles! She didn't even know it was my family's shop until I told her today."

Cora looked at Jeanne, who nodded and said, "*Désolée.* I'm sorry I did not tell you about Leo and me, Cora. I did not think it would matter." Cora huffed a mocking laugh. Jeanne continued, "I did not steal the truffles. I didn't even know Leo was connected to the shop until I told him about our adventure, and he explained the connection today."

Jackson asked, "What *is* the connection between you, Leo?"

Leo tugged at his shirt collar and wondered aloud if they should all sit down. Once Leo and Jeanne were back on the bench and the Doemners around them on the grass, he started: "When my family came over from Poland after the War, they started trading goods, mostly foodstuffs. They, uh, became known for acquiring hard to get items, and eventually, for purchasing hard to sell items." He cleared his throat, and Cora guessed that Leo meant stealing or at least buying stolen goods.

Mr. and Mrs. Doemners eyes got wider. Jackson reached into Cora's backpack and pulled out Cora's sketchbook to take notes. Bradley was actively shredding leaves into confetti.

Jeanne watched Leo quietly. Cora had a hard time figuring out how she felt about this revelation.

"When I graduated from *lycée* — you call it 'high school' — my family decided to help me start on a new path by sending me to culinary school in the States. When I finished, my uncle, whom you met at the shop, introduced me to his friend, Monsieur Bocuse, who hired me as *le entremétier*."

Leo ended his explanation looking at Jeanne, as if silently apologizing. Her eyes were bright with unshed tears.

Cora stared at them. She felt like an idiot. Leo hadn't liked her. Trying to kiss her hand had just been his French way of being nice to a little girl. She couldn't believe she had let her feelings of infatuation blind her from seeing that Leo was obviously connected to the crime. He really should have been her first suspect.

"So why don't we just go ask your uncle who sold him the truffles?" Jackson asked.

Leo shook his head. "No, *mon oncle* would never reveal his source. That's what keeps him in business."

"And he probably doesn't keep written records?" Mrs. Doemner guessed.

He shook his head again. "*Non.* But I could go and review the tape with you. Maybe I would recognize who it is?" He reached out to grab Jeanne's hand and stared into her eyes as he said, "I know it could never be Jeanne."

Cora wanted to throw up. Instead, she turned to the page in her book with the Nowak Shop address. She held it up and said with a grimace, "*Allons-y.*"

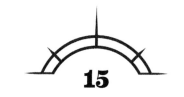

15

CHAPTER QUINZE

ON CANDID CAMERA

Cora spent the entire ride glowering at the world with her arms crossed. Her parents tried to reason with her, but that only made her more agitated. She kept turning around to watch the taxi following them, convinced that Leo and Jeanne were going to use this as a chance to escape.

The taxi finally pulled up to the store and Jackson let out a long sigh of relief. On his way out of the cab, Jackson turned to his sister, "Look Cora, I know this doesn't look good for them. Most of the clues point to them as being the thieves. But, they are here helping us now, so that must mean something." Cora didn't think he sounded like he believed himself.

"Let me take notes. I don't doodle," Jackson said pointing to the swirls covering the margins of her sketchbook. "Only facts." Cora glared at him, but thrust a pencil at him from her pouch.

Cora saw that they were on the same small cobblestone street, only wide enough for one car at a time. The same shops lined the street, and probably the same people walked it. The neighborhood remained unchanged, but Cora felt different. Yesterday she saw this place with eyes of hope and curiosity, convinced that truth would win the day. Today, the dark storm from her ring had found its way overhead. As if the sky itself reflected Cora's bleak mood, a few raindrops fell from gray clouds overhead, splashing onto Cora's nose like the tears she refused to let fall.

Mrs. Doemner took a picture of the opposite wall of a spray-painted Albert Einstein, wearing neon-colored bling. She shouted back at them, "Did you know the earliest art was found here in France? Cave paintings! And since then, France has always been a place of such amazing art! This street art is just so... vivid."

Jackson ran back to the other taxi. After allowing Leo to step out, he pushed in front to offer Jeanne his hand, helping her to the curb. Cora could see that her brother still hoped they were innocent, even though he had suggested they were guilty last night. She felt profoundly alone. Leo opened the door to the shop, and with a wave of his arm, corralled everyone inside out of the rain.

The boy from yesterday still sat at the cash register, as if he had slept there all night. He muttered *"Bonjour"* when they first walked in, but didn't look up until Leo said, *"Salut,* Henri! *Ça va?"*

Henri (which Leo pronounced *"ON-ree"*) looked up in surprise, smiled as he recognized Leo, pulled out his ear buds, and stood up to slap hands. They exchanged the air-cheek-kisses which seemed so weird to Jackson but so normal here in France, and Henri seemed to ask him a string of questions in French. Leo replied in French as well, waving back at his entourage. That's when Henri seemed to notice the rest of them. His face flushed when he spotted Cora. He pointed at her and then at Leo. Cora could see how much Leo and Henri resembled each other, and felt stupid that she hadn't put that together yesterday.

Leo switched to English, "*Oui*, she's with me. We need to see that video tape you showed her."

Henri blushed and he slid his hand into his pocket. Jackson's body tensed as he analyzed the situation. He moved towards Henri. "I see you recognize my sister. But do you recognize her?" Jackson asked, pointing at Jeanne.

Henri shrugged and nodded. "*Oui*, she was with…" he gestured at Cora. "*Bonjour*," he said to Jeanne, almost as an afterthought.

Leo pointed at the video screen. "Can you show us what you showed Cora?" he asked.

Henri glanced at the back door of the shop, which made the Doemners look that way too. Cora remembered being caught in the back room yesterday, and panic surged through her thinking she might get caught snooping around again. At least her parents were with her today. That gave her a small amount of comfort.

Henri explained as he pulled up the file and turned the monitor around so everyone could see: "The camera displays on my screen continuously, but the cloud recording is only triggered by movement, to save memory space. This starts at 5:15," he pointed at the date and time stamp displayed in the bottom right corner.

Jackson noticed that the boy's counter was not in the shot, probably so the cashier wouldn't set off the motion detector, but the rest of the store, from the front door to the back was visible in black-and-white. He looked up at the camera in the corner behind Henri. Based on the weird distortion in the picture and the fact that he could see such a wide range, Jackson guessed it used a fisheye lens.

"Were you here when this happened?" Jackson asked. Cora felt annoyed that her brother was taking over the investigation but stopped herself from interrupting when she remembered that she had quit the job because of Jeanne and Leo's betrayal.

Henri shook his head. "I don't get in until 10:00, when we open," he said.

The group watched the video: an older man with balding white hair emerged from the backdoor, walked to the front door, unlocked it, and let in a woman. She did seem to be carrying a glass jar, though it was hard to tell precisely. The man walked intentionally between her and the camera, but they could still make out her headscarf: black with white polka dots.

Jeanne exclaimed, "I don't own a headscarf with polka dots!"

Cora raised her eyebrow.

Jeanne sensed her skepticism, but it was not until the tape resumed with the woman leaving the back room that he could prove Jeanne's case. "There!" Jeanne pointed at the woman's neck. "Her scarf is tied under her chin, but you can still see her neck and her, uh, *décolletage*..." Jeanne stammered to a stop, bright red as she gestured towards the lady's chest.

Sure enough, the woman's skin showed between the scarf and the top of her blouse.

Cora hasn't even noted that when she watched the video previously. In America, that did not matter. It hadn't even registered that Jeanne might have a different personal standard of dress. She remembered her mom explaining that the *hijab* was for modesty;

Muslim women were only supposed to show their faces and hands in public. If Jeanne was not comfortable showing off her hair in public, she certainly would have covered her neck, too.

Cora's mouth scrunched to one side, considering this new understanding. But Jackson noticed something else. He grabbed Cora's arm while pointing at the screen.

"Jeanne is too tall to be this woman," he said. "Look, Jeanne is wearing flat shoes and her head comes above the tallest shelf." Everyone looked from Jeanne's head to the shelves and back. "But this woman," Jackson pointed back at the tape, "was wearing heels and her head barely reached the top shelf." He asked Henri to rewind the tape to the beginning where you could see high heels peeking out from beneath her skirt and measured her against the shelf behind her.

Leo blew out a loud puff of air. Jeanne beamed at him. "Good eyes, Jackson," Mr. Doemner smiled. Jackson grinned. He could get used to this detective business.

Cora's mouth remained pinched. She was not ready to be convinced. "Henri?" she asked the boy. "Do you recognize this woman?"

Henri squinted and turned his head to one side. He shook his head, "*Non, désolé.*"

Cora put her hands on her hips. "Okay, fine. So Jeanne is only guilty of lying about having a boyfriend," Cora said, releasing most of her anger. Jeanne and Leo moved apart from each other. Cora immediately felt bad for her comment, but wasn't going to admit it.

"This leaves only one suspect," she finished.

Leo looked back at her and asked, "*Qui?* Who is the only suspect?"

"Chef Pierre's sister of course," Cora said, challenging anyone in the room to object.

Jackson rolled his eyes at Cora's obsession.

"Chef Pierre?" Leo asked.

"Yes." Cora explained what Napoleon had seen and her theory that Pierre had smuggled out the truffles in paper bags to his sister, who had come here to sell them.

Leo's eyebrows were furrowed. "I suppose it's plausible. But Chef Pierre has worked for Monsieur Bocuse forever. Even though the truffles were valuable, I don't think they would be worth the risk of losing his job over them. He is paid quite well for his years at the restaurant..." Leo ran his fingers through his hair.

"Listen," Cora continued making her case. "He admitted his sister was having a hard time. Why stop at just giving her food when he could put four-thousand Euros in her pocket... and fire the Muslim girl he hates at the same time?" Cora waved at Jeanne.

That last bit did seem to affect Leo. He looked at Jeanne protectively, remembering Chef Pierre's racist jabs. "He was always short and ill-tempered with Jeanne, but he is with all of us," Leo said. "Chefs are often known for their aggressive demeanor while commanding a kitchen. But you told me he called Jeanne... that word... I was shocked and hurt. I had not known things were so bad. I'm sorry," he said directly to Jeanne, while taking her hands in his.

Cora, forgetting she was mad at the couple, nearly cried at Jeanne's expression. During their investigation, Jeanne had just seemed to brush off the part where the Chef called her that terrible name. To Cora, it seemed she was more concerned about being accused of a crime she didn't commit than being taunted by a bully. But, in that moment, Cora realized that Jeanne had likely just stuffed her hurt deep down so she would not have to feel it. Leo looking at his girlfriend so openly and apologizing seemed to break the wall Jeanne had built to protect herself. She started to softly cry.

"So how would we prove that it was Chef Pierre's sister?" Leo asked, putting his arm protectively around Jeanne's shoulders.

"Aye, there's the rub," Mrs. Doemner said.

Cora sighed. "I have no idea. Dad won't let me steal surveillance footage from the Paris police department. Jackson seems to think it unlikely Chef Pierre will allow his sister to be fingerprinted." She threw her hands up in defeat.

Jackson had an idea. "Dad, can I borrow your phone?"

"Sure," Mr. Doemner said, typing in the password and handing the smartphone to Jackson. "Whacha got in mind?"

"Online search," Jackson muttered. He typed "Pierre Broulliet" into a search bar. He started scrolling through the 92 entries that popped up.

Leo shrugged. "Chef Pierre is a dinosaur. I don't even think he has a smartphone. I can't imagine he's online."

Jackson sighed. He handed the phone back to his dad. "Just restaurant reviews, no pictures or personal social media. I was hoping he might have some family photos online somewhere. Oh well."

As Cora watched her dad slide the phone into his pocket, she asked, "But what about a wallet? Might he have a picture of his sister in his wallet?"

Leo shrugged and turned to Jeanne. "What do you think?" She mirrored him, pulling her shoulders towards her ears. "He might."

Bradley asked, "So how do we steal his wallet?"

Leo and Jeanne looked at each other. "Well, sometimes he changes into his chef's uniform at the restaurant." Leo suggested. "There's a staff locker room where we can keep our stuff."

"Does he lock his locker?" Cora asked.

"Not usually. Doesn't have to. Everyone is too afraid to steal from Chef Pierre." Leo huffed a tight laugh.

"Perfect," Cora said with a mischievous smirk. "What could be more poetic than stealing from a thief?" Cora Joy Doemner was back on the case!

"Ahem," Dad cleared his throat. "Let's make sure there's no stealing. Only observing, ok?"

Cora raised one shoulder, "Tomay-to, tomah-to."

As she started towards the exit, Jackson turned back to Henri. "Could we get a copy of this video?" he asked.

Henri looked at Leo. Leo put his hand on his heart and said something in French, which Cora guessed meant something like, "I'll owe you one," because Henri glanced again at the back door, sighed, and clicked to make a copy. "Who should I email it to?"

Everyone raised their hands.

16

C H A P T E R   S E I Z E

FOLLOW THE PAPER TRAIL

The plan was to wait until Chef Pierre came back from his afternoon "lunch" and then have Leo scope out the locker room. Everyone huddled together behind one of the delivery vans in the back parking lot, right where Napoleon had been eating his lunch the other day. Cora peered through its front windows at the back entrance.

Cora looked down at her watch. 3:30. Chef Pierre should be back any minute.

"What if he goes in the front entrance?" Jackson whispered.

Jeanne shook her head. "No one is allowed in or out the front door while we're closed; it would confuse the patrons."

"Patrons?" Bradley looked up from where he'd been studying ants following a crack in the asphalt.

"Guests," Jeanne explained with a smile.

Bradley nodded and kept trying to shepherd the ants into a new direction with his stick.

"Shh!" Cora hissed. "Here he comes!"

A small red car drove into the back parking lot. "*Non,*" Leo corrected her. "That's the Bocuses's Fiat."

The car pulled into the spot closest to the door, and Monsieur and Madame Bocuse stepped out of the vehicle. Monsieur looked strange without his chef whites, dressed in grey slacks, a black turtleneck and a thigh-length camel-colored coat. Madame looked every inch the French woman, in a dark blue pencil skirt and flowy white blouse, accented by red heels and a red neck scarf. She took her sunglasses off and tucked them into her purse as she followed her husband into the restaurant.

"Is this going to be a problem?" Jackson asked.

Cora looked at Leo who shook his head. "I don't think so," he said, but his voice warbled a bit. Cora wondered if some back-up might be a good idea.

Just then another red car pulled into the parking lot and swept into the spot next to the Bocuses. Cora watched Chef Pierre take a long final swig of Diet Coke from a can, toss it into the back seat, then step out of his vehicle. He reached into the passenger seat to grab his toque, jammed the white hat onto his head, and quickly waddled up the steps into the restaurant.

"Okay," Cora breathed. "Let's go."

"Let's?" Leo asked.

Cora nodded. "Yep, I'm going with you."

All the adults seemed to object at once: "What?" "No way!" "Excuse me??"

"Don't worry! I'll stay hidden!" she reassured them.

But Jackson asked, "Why would you be in the restaurant?"

"You're right," she said. "Mom, Dad? You take the boys around to the front and hang out, like you're waiting for them to open at four. That way, if I'm seen, I can say that I was just, you know, trying to see if we could get a special reservation..." she smiled in her broadest, most self-assured manner.

Mr. and Mrs. Doemner looked at each other, shook their heads and then waved Cora on towards the restaurant in defeat. Cora loved that her parents encouraged independence in their children; she could usually get them on board with her crazy schemes with enough charismatic confidence. They stood up, groaning a bit from sitting on a concrete curb for the last twenty minutes. Mr. Doemner brushed off his trousers and said, "Alright, boys, we're on diversion duty out front."

Mrs. Doemner said to Cora, "Text Dad if you need anything, okay?"

Jackson seemed inclined to follow Cora, but then Bradley would have wanted to come too, so Cora convinced both boys to follow Mom and Dad. Leo helped Jeanne to her feet and held her hand with both of his as he told her something mushy in French.

For a moment, Cora wished a handsome French man were wishing romantic things in her ear, then shook her head. *Don't be ridiculous*, she told herself. *Too gross.*

"Come on!" she whispered vehemently to Leo. "You're not going off to war!"

Leo snorted and Jeanne grinned with a blush. He pecked her quickly on the cheek and followed Cora around the van towards the restaurant. The plan was for Jeanne to stay there and keep watch for anything unusual.

Cora almost giggled as she envisioned Jeanne as their getaway driver, careening around the corner at high-speed in a delivery van.

When they got to the door, Leo paused, his hand on the doorknob. He looked down at Cora. "Okay, I'm going to go in first. If I see anyone, I'll start talking to them, so stay put. If not, I'll wave you in. *Comprends?*"

Cora nodded. She took a deep breath as Leo opened the door and snuck a peek as he walked into the kitchen. He looked around, then back at Cora, waving her to follow.

She slipped in carefully and was about to walk forward when Leo waved her back. She crouched down and hid herself behind a large cardboard box standing in the entryway.

Chef Pierre emerged from the locker room, rolling up the sleeves of his chef's jacket. He looked surprised to find Leo standing in front of him.

"Leo!" Cora heard him exclaim before he launched into some French she didn't understand. She started biting her nails. Whatever Leo said in response evidently worked, because Chef Pierre nodded and absent-midedly pointed back towards the room he'd just left. Then he headed for the dining room. Leo asked him a question and Chef Pierre replied before leaving the kitchen.

"Quick," Leo whispered loudly. "He's gone to check on the tables." He nudged her towards the door and she scooted through it. "I told him I was here looking for my jacket."

The room looked like a long closet with lockers along one side of the wall and a curtained off portion at the end that Cora assumed was for changing one's clothes.

"Which one is Peirre's?" she asked Leo.

He pointed to the end of the row, bottom level. She followed him over. They both stopped. A combination padlock hung from the latch.

"You're sure this is his locker?"

Leo nodded. Cora grabbed her hair. They didn't have time to guess padlock codes! Could she pick the lock? Probably not.

"Grrr!" she roared in frustration, stopping herself from kicking the lockers just in time.

"He probably installed it after the truffle incident," Leo suggested.

Of course. Cora smacked the front of her head. *Think, think, think...* Then she stopped. She remembered her dad warning her about setting the passcode for her suitcase: "Don't use your birthdate," he had said. "It's the most common combination."

"What's his birthday?" Cora asked Leo.

Leo's eyes widened. "I have no idea."

Cora scrunched up her lips. "I bet the Bocuses have it in their records."

"You think he used his birthdate as his lock combination?"

Cora nodded. "Worth a shot. We need to get into their office."

Leo covered his face. "I'm sooo getting fired."

"Don't worry!" Cora said. "Monsieur Bocuse gave us permission to solve the crime. We'll just remind him of that, if necessary," she said as pulled open the door to peek out.

Coast clear.

She pulled the door open so it hid her and she directed Leo through. "After you," she whispered.

Leo shook his head and started towards the Bocuses's office. Just as Cora came out, he dragged her into the crisper beside them.

"What? Hey!" Cora exclaimed.

Leo held his finger to her lips as he pulled the crisper door closed. "Both Madame and Monsieur are in their office. We can't get in there!"

Cora chewed her lip. Then her eyes lit up. She pulled her phone out of her pocket and pushed the speed dial. Her mom answered. "Hey Mom?" she said quietly. "Leo and I need a diversion. Can you call the Bocuses and tell them you're here to say goodbye? ….Yeah, stall them as long as you can. Apologize for not solving the case. Whatever. Great, thanks!"

She hung up and pulled open the door the slightest possible crack. She waited. Leo shivered and rubbed his arms behind her. Her breath fogged her glasses just as she heard the Bocuses's office door open and close. She saw Monsieur and Madame Bocuse walk through the kitchen and out through the dining room, presumably to the front door where her family waited. Hopefully they didn't notice Cora's absence.

She and Leo crept from their hiding place and hurried into the office. She instructed Leo to check the filing cabinets while she searched the desk. Leo pulled open the top drawer and started looking through the manila folders, repeating "Broulliet… Broulliet… Broulliet" under his breath.

She yanked open the bottom desk drawer, not exactly sure where they would keep employees' paperwork. As she rifled through folder after folder of receipts, Cora shook her head. *Man, this woman needs to go paperless!* Cora thought. There were yellow, pink and white receipts jamming every folder all the way to the back. Cora couldn't read them because they were all in French, but she assumed none of them would have Chef Pierre's birthday on them.

She opened the middle drawer. Full of pencils, pens, erasers, White-Out (*White-out! Who used White-Out these days?*) paperclips, staples, rubber bands and other odds and ends. Nope.

She pulled open the top drawer and stopped.

"Got it!" Leo whispered loudly, holding up Chef Pierre's file. He set it on the top of the other files and started searching for the one that would disclose Pierre's birthdate.

"Leo," Cora said, her voice strained. He looked up. "What?"

She pointed into the drawer. "What'd you find?" he repeated.

The look she gave him was enough to make him glance quickly out the window that connected them to the kitchen and come around to her side of the desk.

Lying in the top drawer of the desk was a dark blue and white-polka-dot scarf. Large enough to cover one's whole head. Leo looked at her, "You don't think…?"

Cora shook her head, frozen at the sight of the scarf. "I don't know. It doesn't make any sense!"

Just then, they heard voices. Mr. Doemner spoke extra loudly. "Oh, no, Auguste, we don't want to trouble you!" Cora looked at the filing cabinet and down at the drawer, panicking, but it was too late. Madame Doreen crossed in front of the window and saw both her and Leo standing in her office.

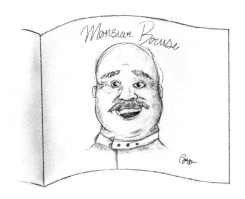

FOILED BY FASHION

"*Merde*," Leo muttered. Cora didn't have to understand what it meant to share the sentiment.

Madame Doreen came into the office, screeching in French and then switching to English, shouting back at the Doemners who were now also standing in front of the window: "What is going on here?"

Mr. and Mrs. Doemner started blushing in embarrassment. "Uh, well, we can explain..."

Cora pulled the scarf from the drawer and held it up to her parents. Her mom gasped and covered her mouth. Mr. Doemner's blush darkened into an angry red.

"*Désolée*, Madame Bocuse," Cora said carefully. "But is this your scarf?"

Madame Doreen nodded impatiently, "*Oui*, but why are you in my office?" She gestured to the filing cabinet and the drawers, "Ransacking my private storage compartments and our confidential employee information?"

Monsieur Bocuse and the rest of the Doemners trailed her into the tiny office.

Cora felt the natural terror of a child facing a loud angry adult, but overcame it with righteous indignation. She took a deep breath. "Well," she said as calmly as Madame Doreen was not, "Monsieur Bocuse authorized me to solve the case of the missing truffles. Which I have now done," she said, holding the incriminating scarf out.

Madame Doreen's red face drained to white. "What... What do you mean?" she asked, choking on the words.

Jackson had the video pulled up on his dad's phone, like he'd been watching it for additional clues. He held it out to Monsieur Bocuse. "Sir, yesterday, we discovered that your truffles were sold to a..." he looked at Leo, then turned back to Monsieur Bocuse, "...local merchant." He pushed play and Monsieur and Madame Bocuse watched the video play.

"But you can't think that I stole my own truffles?" Madame Bocuse exclaimed. "Anyone could have a scarf like that! They sell hundreds at the market."

Bradley had found her purse lying on the chair by the door. He reached in and pulled out her sunglasses, "With sunglasses like this?" He put them onto his face and pranced around, imitating the walk of the woman in the video.

"And pumps like those?" Mrs. Doemner added sadly, pointing

at Madame Bocuse's shoes.

Monsieur didn't even seem to need those reassurances. He seemed to recognize his wife, even from behind, even in disguise. He looked at Madame with a pained expression on his face.

"It was *you*?" he asked.

At that, Madame burst into tears. "Don't look at me like that, Auguste! I did it to save us. To save this!" she held her arms out to the restaurant behind them. "We've never been able to regain our profit margins since the economy crashed, and I wasn't going to be able to pay our employees this week without cash. The insurance would cover the theft. It was all I could think to do."

She reached out to him, as if asking for understanding, but he stepped back. "But why didn't you tell me?"

His rejection must have hurt her, because her sadness switched to anger. "Tell you? I have been telling you! Every week, I've been telling you we cannot continue like this, but you tell me everything will work out!" She raised her voice in a mocking imitation of his words. "But you are not the one who has to balance the books," she pointed an accusatory finger towards the ledger sitting on her desk, "and you are not the one who signs everyone else's paychecks while we go hungry!" she raged.

Cora gulped. She was glad a desk separated her from Madame Doreen. Her dad slowly pushed Mrs. Doemner and the boys behind him.

"Anthony gave me a great deal on those truffles. Enough to get us through another two weeks!" she switched to pleading, hoping her husband would understand.

"And you were willing to let Jeanne go to jail for it?" Leo demanded, his own face flushed scarlet.

"*Non*!" Madame Doreen wailed, clearly distraught. "We would not have pressed charges." She looked at Monsieur Bocuse, "I would have made sure we didn't press charges."

"But you were willing to accept our payment?" Mr. Doemner growled, "AND you were going to take the insurance payment for the loss?"

Cora did not see her dad get angry very often, but he was clearly upset. She knew loyalty and honesty were very important qualities to him.

Madame Doreen looked down at her feet and rubbed her hands. "I am so sorry, Mich'el. I knew it was wrong, but I viewed it as a short-term loan. I figured that if we could survive just another month or so, until the holiday season, we would be fine. As soon as we were back in the black, I had intended to pay you back." She looked at Mr. and Mrs. Doemner with sad eyes. "Truly."

Mrs. Doemner laid a hand on Mr. Doemner's arm and he released his breath. She stepped around him to put a hand on Madame Bocuse's shoulder. "It sounds like you've been having a hard time," she said. Madame Bocuse began sobbing in earnest and Mrs. Doemner grabbed a tissue from the box on the desk. "There, there," she said, wrapping her arms around the woman while Madame Doreen mopped black mascara out of her eyes.

Cora shifted her feet. This was not at all how she thought the case would go. She had liked Madame Doreen (kind of) and the lady seemed really sorry. She looked at her dad. "Now what?" she mouthed.

He shrugged and turned to Monsieur Bocuse. "It sounds like a little cash might help alleviate some of the pressure around here... Why don't you show me what's been going on and we'll talk about turning that, uh, four-thousand Euro *loan* into something a little more official?"

Monsieur Bocuse's eyes filled with tears at that, and he nodded, with his lips pressed together. "Leo?" he turned. "Could you see if any of Victor's *Tarte Tatin* is left over from lunch? I'm sure the Doemners would love some served over *la glace*."

Leo nodded, and that action reminded Cora of Jeanne. "So, does this mean Jeanne can have her job back?" she asked. Monsieur looked at his wife and then said, "Of course."

"Yes!" Cora pumped her fist and headed out of the office. She ran to the back door and shouted across the parking lot: "Jeanne! Come here!"

The older girl raced from her hiding place, concern etched on her face. "Is everything okay?"

Cora took a deep breath. "I guess so? It's complicated," she responded, pulling Jeanne into the kitchen. She started to explain the most recent developments when they came face to face with Chef Pierre. His chest puffed up and Cora thought of a rooster, fluffing up his feathers as he prepared to attack. "Hey Chef Pierre!" Cora exclaimed with a big smile on her face before he had a chance to say anything. "We proved Jeanne was innocent and Monsieur Bocuse said Jeanne could have her job back! Isn't that GREAT NEWS?" she emphasized the last two words, as if willing him to agree with her.

She watched his chest deflate, his forehead creased with a confused expression. He looked over at the office where the Bocuses and Mr. and Mrs. Doemner were huddled over the desk.

Cora led Jeanne past the bewildered chef and out to the dining room where Leo sat with the boys. Leo turned and swept Jeanne into a big hug. "Did Cora tell you?" he asked. "You're cleared!" He smiled down at Cora. "Well, I guess *we* are cleared, since evidently we were the primary suspects." Cora blushed to the tops of her ears and said, "I didn't get to the details."

Leo held out a chair for Jeanne to sit down and said, "Well, do fill her in. I'll be back with refreshments," and he returned to the kitchen.

Cora walked Jeanne and her brothers through what had happened. Jackson was impressed that she had thought of using Chef Pierre's birthdate. Bradley made sure Jeanne knew he had produced the sunglasses at a key moment in the case.

"So," Cora finished. "Evidently, the Bocuses were short on cash and Madame Doreen decided to sell the truffles. I guess she didn't realize you would get blamed. She's sorry and Monsieur Bocuse said you could have your job back."

Leo caught this last part as he backed through the swinging doors carrying a tray with five plates of warm apple tart, each with a heaping scoop of vanilla ice cream on top. He passed out the plates with spoons, saying, "Isn't that great, Jeanne? You and I could work together again!" He grinned down at her.

Cora didn't realize that Chef Pierre had followed them into the dining room. His face was beet red, clearly angry. Before anyone could stop him, he came within inches of Jeanne's face, screaming and showering her in a spray of spit. "I do not know what trick you have done, how you have convinced these people of your innocence, but you do NOT fool me. I do NOT want someone like YOU in my kitchen." He turned the word "YOU" in his mouth like it was a sour grape.

"PIERRE!" Monsieur Bocuse stood in the doorway, having run from the office to investigate the commotion in the dining room.

Chef Pierre, not missing a beat, turned to his boss, "You let this… girl… back into MY KITCHEN?"

"Pierre, that is enough." Now it was Madame Doreen speaking. She looked tiny compared to her husband, but Cora noticed she held her head high as she confessed, "I took the truffles, it was me." She stepped forward to place her body in between Jeanne and the red-faced Chef.

"It is not YOUR kitchen. It is MY kitchen," Monsieur Bocuse clarified. "I trained you. I taught you everything you know. You learned under my wing and my tutelage. I absolutely will not tolerate your treatment of Jeanne." Monsieur Bocuse had moved his wife out of the line of fire and now stood toe to toe with the tiny chef.

Jeanne looked shocked. Cora ran to her side and wrapped her arms around her waist, filled with regret over being angry at her beautiful friend. Cora realized that she had no experience that compared to Jeanne's. Cora would never fully know what it felt like to live as a foreigner in her own homeland, or be hated by people because of her skin color or religion, but she caught a glimpse of that awful reality now. The injustice of it all smacked her in the face, and Cora felt so helpless. All she could do was stand by her friend and show that she supported her.

"I think, sir, that it is time for you to pack your things and go." Monsieur Bocuse pointed to the backroom that was filled with lockers.

Pierre stood, frozen.

Peeling Cora's arms off of her, Jeanne stood up. "Please, sir," she said to Monsieur Bocuse. "I am tired of standing by and saying nothing."

Madame Bocuse grabbed the girl's hand, "Jeanne, it's okay. Let Monsieur Bocuse handle it."

"No," Jeanne said firmly but kindly, "I will use my voice thank you."

Everyone in the room moved aside to allow Jeanne to move towards the shrinking Chef Pierre. Cora knew that no one in this room would allow Jeanne to be harmed or silenced. Even Bradley and Jackson stood at the ready, fists clenched, ready for a brawl. She watched her friend fill with clarity and confidence. She moved even closer to the quivering man. "I am sorry your heart is so small. I will no longer allow your words, your attitude, or your malice affect me. You can choose hate, but I choose love." She held out her hand.

Chef Pierre clearly did not know what to do. He looked at Monsieur Bocuse. Monsieur Bocuse shrugged and stepped back, giving the Chef a chance to make amends.

Chef Pierre looked at the young girl in front of him, standing tall, willing to forgive his cruelty. He chewed on his teeth, trying to digest a new idea. But evidently the prospect of a future in which he was wrong got caught in his throat, because he spun on his heel and stormed out of the dining room.

Cora released the breath she'd been holding. Jeanne dropped her hand and raised her shoulders, letting the Chef and her resentment go. The air in the dining room felt like a spring day after a thunderstorm.

"Leo," Monsieur Bocuse exclaimed, clapping the young man on the shoulder, "I trained Chef Pierre. I can train you. How would you like to be my head Chef-in-training?"

Leo looked at his boss in amazement, and nodded. "*Oui... Merci*, Monsieur! I will not let you down!" He turned to Jeanne elated. "Jeanne, we can work here together!"

Jeanne smiled shyly back at him, and said, "Well, actually, Mrs. Doemner and I were chatting and she thinks she can get me a job as a docent at the *Musée d'Orsay*."

"What's a docent?" Bradley asked, mouth full of tarte, lips covered in ice cream.

"A tour guide at a museum," Jeanne explained. "In this case, a gorgeous art museum, built in a romantic old train station and filled with my very favorite impressionist art, including Van Gogh's *Starry Night*..." Jeanne trailed off like she was in a dream, her hands folded over her heart, her eyes raised towards the heavens.

Jackson looked at her with eyebrows raised. "You would rather walk around a train station talking about art than make food with your boyfriend?"

Leo seemed equally bemused by her decision.

Jeanne reached out to cover Leo's hand. "Of course I love spending time with Leo," she said to Jackson, "But not at work. It has been too hard keeping things secret between us. Plus, this whole experience has helped me to realize that while I enjoy cooking for my family and friends," she smiled at the Doemner children, "But I don't really enjoy the fast pace of a commercial kitchen." She paused and then said, "I guess you can say this incident has left a bad taste in my mouth for cooking, but it has also given me the confidence to do what I really want to do in my life."

Jeanne shined brightly at everyone standing in a circle around her. Mrs. Doemner walked up to her and hugged her tightly.

"You're practically a Doemner now," Bradley joked, holding up a spoonful of dessert. "We spend a lot of time staring at art!"

Mrs. Doemner put her arm around the girl's shoulders. "Welcome to the family."

18

CHAPTER DIX-HUIT

THE WORLD, MY HOME

It was their last night in Paris and Cora had to spend it at a stuffy, boring art event. She groaned. The museum where her mother had authenticated the art had decided to throw a gala to celebrate their new acquisition. Cora had been instructed to "dress nicely." A scratchy chiffon dress lay on her hotel bed. She sighed and briefly considered throwing it out the hotel window.

"Hurry up, sweetie, put the dress on!" Mrs. Doemner called through the door.

Cora gritted her teeth and squeezed into the fancy dress. Sitting on the edge of the bed, she buckled her shiny black mary janes over her white stockinged feet. Her mother came at her with a brush and a look that said *don't you dare object* and started pulling Cora's long unruly blonde locks into two thin brains on either side of her face.

It's just a few hours, Cora told herself as she packed the teal knapsack with her sketchbook and collection of pencils. Resigning herself to the discomfort, she followed her brothers and parents out of the hotel room, through the lobby, to a waiting taxi on the street outside.

They drove through the streets of Paris to the Petit Palais Museum. The streets were busy and bustling in the cool evening air. They passed several outdoor markets, with vendors selling long bolts of fabric, vegetables and fruit, and crusty golden lengths of bread. Cora's mouth watered, imagining yellow butter and strawberry jam on slices of fresh *baguette.*

The taxi pulled up in front of the Petit Palais, and Cora thought it was well-named. It really did look like a small palace. "Now I could live here," she said to her parents.

"It wasn't a real palace," Mrs. Doemner explained. "They built this to house art in 1900 for the World's Fair."

Despite her determination to hate the Gala, Cora was dazzled. The front steps swept up to three concentric arches with columns holding sculpted angels, their wings outstretched, and the Doemners walked through a golden gate to the foyer.

"Ah, Madame Doemner, Monsieur Doemner," called out a small woman in a tight maroon suit jacket, with a straight skirt that fell all the way to the ground underneath her. She clutched a clipboard in her wrinkled hands, her hair pulled back so tightly into a *chignon* that it actually stretched back the skin on her face, making her look continuously vexed. "*Allons-y,* let's go! Zee speakers begin shortly! Everyone eez so excited to hear you talk about your experiences in zee arts!"

Noticing the children trailing behind their mother, the woman snapped to attention. "Ah, you have brought your children I see. Oh well. Children, I do hope you know how to sit still?"

Bradley opened his mouth with a sharp inhale. Mr. Doemner gently placed one hand on his shoulder and one hand on his mouth and brought him close into a backwards hug. The woman looked Bradley up and down with a disapproving stare. "Follow me! Now pleaze!" She commanded with a French accent.

"FAH-LOO ME PLEEEEAAZZZZE..." Bradley whispered under his breath while imitating the woman's prim and proper walk. Mr. and Mrs. Doemner suppressed a laugh.

The Doemners entered a simple gallery with wood floors and red walls. Paintings lined the walls, but nothing like the Louvre. This felt quieter, calmer, more like a very fancy home. Cora relaxed a little.

There were lines of chairs in two sections in front of a makeshift podium. *Ugh, speeches before eating?* Cora felt her stomach grumble, the crepe with strawberries from lunch long gone. She wondered if others could hear the murmurs coming from her belly.

"There will be food as soon as the presentation is over, guys," Mrs. Doemner said as if reading Cora's mind.

They settled into the seats, and Cora pulled out her sketchbook. The speakers got up one by one, talking about things like a damaged painting from a church, the financial needs of the organization, and finally Mrs. Doemner stepped onto the stage to talk about the history of the painting she'd authenticated. Applause filled the room as the Director of the Museum pulled the curtain back to reveal the new painting that had officially been added to the museum's collection.

Mrs. Doemner stepped down from the podium. The woman in the maroon suit came to the microphone and said, "And now ladies and gentlemen, I preezent to you — Sir Theodore Courteney Devré.

He is zee wonderful *philanthropist* who made tonight possible. Pleeze geev heem a warm welcome!"

Everyone stood up and clapped as a large figure jumped up every other stair to the podium. He wore a black tuxedo and his silver hair shone against the dark fabric. Beaming at the audience, he looked right at Cora and waved. Her heart skipped a beat. *Is that...?*

Stunned, she realized that the philanthropist on the stage was the man she had met at the Louvre. The man who had admired her ring and asked about her dad. He looked more refined and distinguished in his tuxedo, but he still wore the same glasses, two huge circles on each side of his nose.

He started talking about his research. He described a group of artists, archaeologists, historians, and geologists dedicated to finding and preserving rare and valuable minerals and stones from all over the world. He had sponsored tonight's event in hopes that each of these distinguished guests might think of him and his work whenever they encountered any pieces of art made with or depicting gems and stones. He was determined to catalogue every known piece of art involving minerals.

Cora remembered her anxiety and shook her head. So, he wasn't a creepy stalker after all. He really had just wanted to meet another archaeologist.

After the speeches concluded, they were finally released to fill small plates with dried sausages, grapes, and cheese with a thick white rind. Cora watched the tall man walk up to her mother. Cora stuffed a bite of *brie* into her mouth and ran up to the two of them.

Mrs. Doemner saw Cora, "Sir Devré, this is my daughter, Cora!"

The man's eyes twinkled. "Well, *bonjour, Mademoiselle artiste.*"

Cora blushed.

Mrs. Doemner looked at both of them, confused.

"I had the pleasure of running into Cora at the Louvre several days ago," the man explained. "She is very talented!"

"Cora didn't tell me..." Mrs. Doemner frowned at her daughter.

"I am sure that meeting an old man like me blathering about gemstones in a museum was not the highlight of her day," his eyes flashed bright green like the emeralds Cora had drawn. "But it turns out that her conversation WAS the highlight of my day," he went on. "Thanks to her, I discovered that you and your husband are very accomplished in your respective fields and perfectly suited to help me with my little project."

"Oh?" Mrs. Doemner asked.

"Yes," Sir Devré responded. "For many years I have been searching for several ancient stones, and recently, I found what I believe may be the first of its kind. If you are amenable, I would like to enlist you and your husband — really, your whole family," he smiled at Cora, "to help me analyze my findings. The excavation is in Guatemala. I would pay you double your current day rate and cover all your travel expenses. I'm afraid things are rather urgent. I would like you to join me there at your earliest convenience."

Mrs. Doemner looked like a deer caught in the beam of a headlight. Cora nudged her mom with her elbow, and she blinked. "Well, yes, of course, that sounds incredible. May I discuss it with my husband...?" she gestured over to Mr. Doemner who was wiping custard off Bradley's face.

"Of course!" Sir Devré beamed. "Yes, please, I'd love to talk to him as well."

As her mom walked in a daze back to their table, Cora became very self-conscious. She cleared her throat and asked politely, "So, uh, where do you live, Sir Devré?"

"Please call me Teddy," the man grinned. "And while I have houses in several countries, I consider the whole world my home. I belong wherever I am standing."

Cora's eyes flew to Teddy's face. Her family traveled a lot and she had never felt like any place was really home. But if Teddy thought of the whole world as his home, maybe she could, too. She liked that idea, and decided at last that she liked Teddy, too.

"You mentioned some stones," she ventured. "What kind of stones are you looking for?"

Teddy's face grew serious and his eyes gazed out, as if seeing far beyond the walls of the room. Finally, he looked down at her. "Magical ones," he said, very quietly.

Cora started to laugh but he didn't look like he was joking. She opened her mouth for a questioning retort, when her parents walked up.

"Sir Devré, may I introduce my husband, Michael?" Mrs. Doemner said as she walked up and Mr. Doemner held out his hand.

They began to discuss the details of the expedition, and Cora overheard something about a mask in the jungle, but all she could think about was Teddy's answer. *Magic stones?* What could he have meant? She wondered if he had just blown her off, thinking she was a child, but she could not shake the notion that Teddy had been telling her the truth, possibly a secret.

Cora snapped out of her reverie as Teddy shook Mr. and Mrs. Doemner's hands saying, "Well that settles it then. I will have my assistant arrange everything and send you the details."

Turning his attention to Cora, the tall man with the silver hair leaned down until he was eye-to-eye with her, "I'm so glad we ran into each other, Cora." She smiled hesitantly. Then he stood up and nodded to her family. "I'm afraid I must be off, but I look forward to seeing you very soon in Flores!" Then he turned and walked quickly out of the Petit Palais with his assistant hopping behind him like a rabbit trying to keep up.

"So, what does that all mean?" Cora asked as they all watched him walk away.

"Well, I guess it means we're going to Guatemala…" Mr. Doemner raised his eyebrows at Mrs. Doemner who nodded. "Oh yes, definitely," she said, rubbing her hands together in glee.

"There's another mystery to solve?" Bradley asked.

"Most likely," his dad said, "but it sounds like this is an ancient mystery."

Cora's eyes started to sparkle. "Can we be official detectives?" she asked.

"Well, I think you can be detectives in training," Mr. Doemner replied. "The best place to learn is on the job. Mom and I would be honored to have you as assistants in our work. There will always be mysteries to solve, no matter where we are."

"What about school?" Jackson interjected.

"Looks like you guys will be homeschooling for a while," Mrs. Doemner said.

"Wait, we aren't going to go back to school?" Bradley exclaimed.

"Not in a classroom, at least not while we are travelling. But trust me Jackson, you will learn plenty while we're abroad. Like Dad said, education is really just solving the mysteries of life," Mrs. Doemner encouraged him.

Cora thought for a moment and remembered Teddy's voice: *The whole world is my home.* She supposed if the whole world could be their home, then the whole world could also be their school. This prospect excited Cora. She looked at her ring. It glowed blue and green like a globe. The whole world on her finger.

"We'll need a name for our school," Cora said, still mesmerized by her ring.

Bradley threw out with a hopeful face, "How about 'Play all Day Never Do Any Work School'?!"

Mr. and Mrs. Doemner shook their heads an adamant NO.

"Nuh uh," Jackson nixed it. He rubbed his chin. "Well, our last name is Doemner, so... Doemner Academy?"

"No, this is bigger than us. It's the whole world," Cora said.

"And we're solving mysteries instead of going to school!" Bradley added.

Mrs. Doemner smiled, "So what do you think of the Doemner World Mystery Academy?"

Cora pulled out her sketchbook and sketched a banner that read "Doemner World Mystery Academy" and held it up for inspection. "This could be our emblem!"

"We're going to need school t-shirts," Bradley said, "And a website. Oh, and teachers. Is Dad the principal? Or the nurse? Oh dear — who is the lunch lady?"

Mr. Doemner laughed, "I think your mother and I are all of those things!"

While Cora's family continued on talking about how the Doemner

World Mystery Academy would handle things like gym class, report cards, and recess (art class was totally covered), Cora got lost in the spinning globe on her hand. What started as a short trip to France, had now turned into an epic adventure. She was going to a place she had never heard of or even imagined she would go. *Guatemala.*

Cora decided, no matter where they went, she would make the whole world her home.

Fin

FRENCH GLOSSARY

Adieu - "Goodbye"

Allons y - "Let's go!"

Artiste - Artist

Au revoir - "Good-bye" - literally, "Till we see (each other) again!"

À votre service - "At your service" (usually in response to "Thank You")

Bien sûr - "Of course!"

Bonjour - Literally "Good (*bon*) day (*jour*)," this is the easiest way to say hello at all times of day.

Boucher - Butcher

Ça va? - "How's it going?"

C'est combien? - "How much does this cost?"

C'est très magnifique - "It is very magnificent"

C'est pas possible! - "That's not possible!"

Cinq - five. French numbers 1- 10 are "un, deux, trois, quatre, cinq, six, sept, huit, neuf, dix." You can Google the pronunciation on YouTube!

De rien - technically "It's nothing," the French use it the way we say "You're welcome" - in response to someone thanking them

Décolletage - a low neckline on a woman, or the skin exposed by such a neckline

Désolé / Désolée - "I'm sorry." If you are a male, you write it with one accented "e"; if you are female, you write it with two e's, and accent the first. But they're both pronounced "*deh-zo-LAY.*"

Enchanté / Enchantée - While the literal translation is "enchanted," it means "nice to meet you." If you are a male, you write it with one accented "e"; if you are female, you write it with two e's, and accent the first. But they're both pronounced "*on-shon-TAY.*"

Fleuriste - florist

Gastronomie - related to cuisine; a shop that sells delicacies

Encore - "Again" — you'll hear it at concerts and other performances; if the artist is very good, the audience will shout "*Encore!*" asking for more.

Entremétier - A cook responsible for preparing hot appetizers, soups, vegetables, pasta, and starches

Excusez moi - "Excuse me"

Fin - "The End"

Fraternité - in English we say "Fraternity" which you can think of as "Brotherhood" or a spirit of friendship and mutual support.

Garçon - your waiter at a restaurant

Je comprends – (zhə com–prawn) – "I understand" (also, see: "*Tu comprends?*" down below)

Je m'appelle... - "My name is…"

Je suis - "I am"

Jolie fille - pretty girl

Lycée - (lie-SEE) French public high school

Madame - the title for a married woman, like "Mrs."

Mademoiselle - the title for an unmarried girl or woman, like "Miss."

Mesdemoiselles - plural; more than one "mademoiselle"

Monsieur - the title for a man, like "Mr."

Mes amis - "my friends." *Mon Ami* is the singular - "my friend"

Merci - While it literally translates "mercy", it's pronounced "mehr-SEE." It means "Thank You."

Merci beaucoup means "Thank you very much." and is pronounced "mehr-SEE bow-COO"

Maman - "Mama"

Métro - An underground train that carries people around central Paris.

"Métro" is short for "Métropolitan" which means "Big City" ("Polis" is the Greek word for "City" - a root you'll find in other words like "Politician").

Merde - a bad word, roughly translated, "Ah, Poop."

Mon - ("mohn" - the N is almost silent) - "my" if the thing you're referring to is masculine; *Ma is* "My" if the thing you're referring to is feminine

Mon dieu! - Technically "My God!" It's a typical French phrase that can be used to express lots of emotions, from horror to surprise to exasperation.

"N'importe quoi!" - (nim-poor-to-kwah) "That's crazy!"

Non - No

Oui - pronounced "whee", this means "yes" in French

Oncle - (to pronounce this word, pinch your nose and say "awn-cluh") - "Uncle"

Papa - "Daddy"

Parlez vous anglais? (PAR-ley vooz ON-glay) - "Do you speak English?"

petit fils - grandson; *petit fille* - granddaughter.

Pourquoi? - (Poor-QWA) - "Why?"

Pourquoi cherchiez-vous dans mon réfrigérateur? - "Why were you looking in my refrigerator?"

Puis-je vous aider? - "How may I help you?"

Produits Régionaux - Regional Products (Latin-based languages tend to put the descriptors after the nouns)

Qui - Who

Qu'est-ce que tu fais? - "What are you doing?"

Qui êtes-vous? - "Who are you?"

Reçu - Receipt

Salut - hello (and sometimes "bye")

S'il vous plaît - please

Sœur - sister

Tu comprends? (too-com-prawns) - "Do you understand?"

Comprenez-vous? - (Com-pron-eh-VOO) would be the more formal way to ask that question.

Un peu - "a little"

Voila! - (VOOWAH-lah) "There it is!" Usually a one-word exclamation, proclaimed as you reveal something spectacular.

Voulez-vous - "Would you...?"

Venir ici - "Come here"

Vraiment? - "Is this true?" In older English, people used to ask "Verily?" in a similar manner

AUTHOR'S NOTE

My dearest Reader,

You are holding a very unusual kind of story, one that includes both facts and fiction. Paris, France is a real place. The historical details we discuss in the book are as true as my research would allow (feel free to correct me if I missed something!).

Many things are fiction: the story's events and its characters are completely imaginary! But the Doemner Family is a mixture of Real-And-Not-Real. You see, I am both the author of the story and a character in the story.

Caitlin, Michael, Cora, Jackson and Bradley Doemner are the names of five real people who happen to enjoy traveling and learning about other cultures. You can follow their real adventures at www.AllOverTheMap.Family.

If you are curious about what else is "Real or Not," you can check out our website: www.WorldMysteryAcademy.com.

If you have questions about the story or our travels, you can email us at Questions@WorldMysteryAcademy.com! We would love to hear from you!

May you discover that every day
      wherever you are
            is an adventure,

C.S. Doemner

ACKNOWLEDGEMENTS

I am so grateful to the many, many people who contributed their time and talents to bring this book to light! No author publishes alone, and in my case, it took an entire village to birth this creative brainchild.

First, to Jacqueline Myers who coached me through the earliest stages of gestation, guiding this non-fiction author through the complexities of crafting her first children's mystery novel.

To Rebecca Dragon, my amazing developmental editor and writing partner, who brought France and these characters alive! You held my hand and kept me focused, driving the project forward even when my life got hard.

To Jude Dragon, Rebecca's 15 year old son, who agreed to illustrate the book while in school. All of the interior drawings were done by hand, by a kid! I'm so proud to feature some of the earliest works of this talented up-and-coming artist.

To my "undercover agents" who agreed to read the first draft and give me feedback, including Emmy, Jamie, and Josiah. I especially want to thank the Illustrious Ella, age 9, who not only gave me line-by-line recommendations, but who also came up with the title of the book!

To Jamie, Shari, Kristen, and Jessica who ran their sharp eyes over every word of the text, helping me catch as many typos as possible!

To Rebecca Card-Hyatt, for her practical suggestions to navigate culturally-treacherous waters with as much accuracy and grace as possible.

To my encouraging Writer's Club, especially Amy Walker, who showed me what it looks like to run a business, raise kids, and pursue one's dreams of being a fictional author all at the same time!

To my editor, Merav Richter, who pulled together all the pieces of the story.

To my publicists, Stephanie Moon and Tara Lewis, who saw an even bigger vision for the books than I, and gave me a roadmap to share these books with the world.

To my art director, Kristine Brogno, for translating my paralyzed artistic perfectionism into a professional, captivating finished product.

To David Marval for coordinating schedules and managing the project. Keeping me sane is a full-time job!

And last but not least, to the real Mr. Doemner, whose patience and encouragement make all of this possible. You are the most incredible man I've ever met and I'm so honored to be on this Journey with you!

ABOUT THE AUTHOR

C.S. Doemner loves writing books that get children excited about travel by immersing them into different cultures. She and her family are currently traveling the world for two years, visiting sixty-five countries and all seven continents. As such, she decided to use her own family as the foundation for her story's characters in her new middle-grade release, *World Mystery Academy: Pursuit in Paris*, the first in a series of books featuring culturally-complicated mysteries around the world.

C.S. Doemner gets inspiration for her stories from the many places around the world she is currently visiting with her husband and three young children. Often when Doemner writes, it feels as if she is writing down a movie that is playing out in her head, and it is being described to her as she types.

An entrepreneur, artist, published author, wife, and mom, C.S. Doemner studied literature and philosophy at Biola and Oxford University. When she isn't writing world-traveling adventure mysteries for children, Doemner is an entrepreneur, enjoys snorkeling, rock climbing, drawing and painting, traveling, watching movies, and reading. Back home, the Doemners have a gigantic black cat named Bagheera and a golden hamster named Hammy.

C.S. Doemner is also the published author of three non-fiction adult books. *World Mystery Academy: Pursuit in Paris* is her debut children's novel.

Printed in Great Britain
by Amazon